HIS STAKES

BY

ANGEL RAYNE

Published by Everblood Publishing, LLC
https://everbloodpublishing.com

ISBN-13: 9781945499616

Cover Design by Maria Christine Pagtalunan @ https://artscandarebookcoverdesign.com/

Copy Editor: Mackenzie @ NiceGirlNaughtyEdits.com

ALSO BY ANGEL RAYNE

Mafia Romance Reading Order

Luca and Veda

His Game

His Stakes

His Win

SYNOPSIS

I knew this game I played might cost me my life.
But I never thought it would cost me my heart.
Until Veda Calbert came into my world.

Granted, I dragged her here kicking and screaming. Took
her from her home to be a pawn in my revenge. I swore
she would never be anything else to me. But somewhere
along the way, she crawled under my skin.
And now, damaged by the time spent with my brother,
both physically and mentally, Veda is determined to hate
me. And I deserve it.
But I won't accept it.

The rules may have changed, but I haven't lost yet.
Because I'm not just giving in to my obsession.
I'm raising the stakes.

CHAPTER 1
LUCA

I *can't breathe. I can't fucking breathe...*

The attacks have been coming more and more frequently since Veda was ripped out of my life. I gripped the arms of the chair I sat in, the brown leather stiff and cold under my fingers as the walls closed in on me. Squeezing my eyes shut, I fought for breath.

My father's angry voice broke through my panicked haze. "You are a disgrace to this family and no son of mine."

His words slid over me but didn't stick, not like they once would have. I was barely paying attention, my mind on that morning. I'd woken up still half-dressed, each beat of my pulse like a hammer chiseling away at my skull, and my sheets stained with the blood that covered me. Blood that wasn't my own. Blood I had no recollection of. I didn't even remember leaving the house.

He paced around his desk and came to stand in front of me. "Are you listening to me, *coglione?*"

I finally gave him my attention. "I'm *not* an idiot."

"*Si'*, you are! How could you just let your brother get away like that?" He walked away, his hands flying through the air in front of him, punctuating every word. "You had one job, Luca. One fucking job! To draw your brother out into the open and bring him here alive. That's it! Instead, you shoot him. You let that fucking thing hanging between your legs do all the thinking for you. Again!" With a disgusted sound, he threw up his hands.

"If you're so disappointed in me, why don't you call in one of my cousins to do the job?" I spat the words out without thinking. The last thing I wanted was for one of my demented cousins to get their hands on Veda, if my brother hadn't already figured out who she really was.

She's alive. She has to be alive.

"So I can listen to your *zio* tell me how he told me so? How he knew from the time he was ten that Mario couldn't be trusted? Ehhh..." He spit on the floor beside my shoe. "Fuck that. Besides, this is family business. Our family. No one else needs to hear anything except what they need to know." He paused. Took a breath as he looked off into the distance. "Mario's always been easily swayed. I've known that his whole life. It's the reason I never let him in on any of the tricky jobs." He shrugged. "He can't help the way he is, but he's still my oldest."

"He's a fucking rat," I told him. Lifting my eyes to his, I purposely kept Veda out of the conversation. "There's only one outcome here, *papa*. All you have to do is give me the nod."

"He's *my son.* Your *fratello—*"

"And he's putting the entire family in danger."

"He's my son," he repeated firmly. "And I'm the boss of this family. Nothing happens to Mario without my permission."

"I'm your son, too!" I raged, unable to keep my temper under control when he was being so blatantly obstinate.

His voice rose to match mine. "And that does not give you the right to ignore my orders! Instead, you chose to save a *woman!* A *WOMAN!*"

The word was said like Veda was no better than a slug, a toy for men like us to use, readily available and no good for anything except sucking our cocks until we tired of them. Blood surged hot in my veins and pounded through my skull, but I refused to give him the satisfaction of knowing how much his words affected me. "I did. Because Veda is innocent in all of this. I never should have dragged her into this sick game. It was stupid of me."

Again, he threw up his hand in disgust, waving away my argument like he always did. "You were going to kill her anyway as soon as you found out she wasn't her sister. Don't give me that bullshit."

Was I? It was true, I'd told myself that, but I didn't fucking know anymore.

"All you did was use the opportunity she presented to you. And probably had a little fun along the way, eh? Nothing wrong with that."

I should have. I should've just followed my father's plan and put a bullet in her head in front of my brother. It was the compromise he had given me, a chance to defend my honor and draw out Mario at the same time, and I'd never faltered from that plan no matter how she'd chipped away at the ice around my heart. Not until the moment came...when she'd stood there staring at me through a stranger's fake blue eyes...compassion and acceptance written all over her beautiful face.

And I just...I couldn't fucking do it.

My father watched me expectantly, but I couldn't tell him what was going through my head. He would tell me I was weak. That I wasn't worth the position he had me in. And you know what? Maybe he was right. But at least I wasn't a fucking rat. I would never do anything to threaten the lives of my family. "Mario needs to be dealt with. You know it as well as I do. If this was anyone else, they'd already be in the ground, and we wouldn't be sitting here arguing about it."

Placing both hands on the arms of my chair, he leaned over me. The smell of whiskey and Brute aftershave washed over me, bringing with it memories of my childhood, when he would try to intimidate me into telling him whatever he wanted to know. Or make me do things I didn't want to do. It didn't work then, and it wouldn't work now. "*I* will deal with your brother, as soon as you fucking find him again. I want him brought to me alive, Luca. *Capeesh?"*

I met his cold, dark eyes. "Yeah, I understand."

He straightened, staring at me a moment before he fixed his tie and walked back around his desk, taking a seat in his oversized chair. Grabbing his cigar box, he chose one and snipped the end before sticking it in his mouth. "Let me know when you find him. And do what you want with the woman. Kill her. Don't kill her. I don't give a *fuck* at this point. She did what we brought her here to do. Mario is no longer hiding out in witness protection. But you need to hurry, before the fucking FBI gets involved again, or one of the other families sees him and takes matters into their own hands. It wasn't just us who he put in a...compromising position." He lit the end of his cigar, puffing a few times. Plumes of fragrant smoke floated around him and burned the inside of my nose. "Just make sure that bitch's mouth is shut permanently when you're finished with her, or I swear to god I'll take care of her myself. We can't have a loose end running around out there." He waved his hand that was holding the cigar, indicating the world in general.

Anger seethed within me. I deserved the chance to take out my brother. Blood be damned. My father had no right to take that away from me. But nothing would make him change his mind when he was all riled up like this. I would have to bide my time and try arguing my case again at a later time. Although I understood his hesitation. I did. Mario was my brother. We grew up together. And there was a time I even looked up to him. But that was long ago, when he wasn't the man he was now.

Standing up, I fastened the buttons on my suit jacket. "I'll let you know as soon as I find him."

He didn't bother to respond as I saw myself out.

Tristan and Enzo were waiting for me in the foyer. Without a word, Tristan opened the door and stepped outside, scanning my father's front yard as Enzo and I followed behind him and got into the SUV. It wasn't until we were on the road back to the lake house that Enzo spoke up.

"How did it go?"

I stared out the window. "He wouldn't do it."

"And Veda?" Tristan asked from the back.

"I can do whatever I want with her, so long as I can get her back while keeping Mario alive for my father to deal with."

Enzo turned on his blinker and eased out onto I-35. "Did he tell you anything else?"

"No."

"What are you going to do? With Mario, I mean," Tristan clarified. He knew me well enough to know I'd taken about all that I would take, despite my father's orders.

"Whatever I have to."

They fell silent, and I took a deep breath, glad for the reprieve. I would get Veda back alive. And I would do whatever I had to do to make it happen.

Fuck my father.

Please. Please, Veda. My vita. *Still be alive.*

CHAPTER 2

VEDA

O*ne Week Earlier...*

He was watching me. He was always watching me.

I tried to ignore his hostile stare as I made him a cup of coffee. Black with a few drops of cream, but not too much, just the way he liked it.

Just the way my sister would've made it for him.

I was informed of this fact just a few minutes ago when I'd had the *audacity* to ask him how he liked his drink. As I poured the freshly brewed coffee with a shaking hand, the side of my face throbbed where the back of his fist had connected, and I knew my cheek was swelling. I could tell even without a mirror because of how tight my skin felt. There was probably a bruise, too. If not now, then soon.

Unfortunately, the everything-feels-so-good drugs Luca had given me at the club had worn off long ago, so I'd felt the hit with every fiber of my being. The stars that danced in front of my eyes were the prelude to a raging headache that made my skull feel like it was splitting apart every time I moved.

So yeah, they'd long since worn off, but I still used them as an excuse for forgetting such a simple thing as how he liked his coffee.

"Nicole! Hurry it the fuck up with that. I have things to do."

Was this the way he'd treated my sister? Was this the reason why she'd never told me about him?

Or was he just fucking with me, because he knew I wasn't really her?

My eyes burned from the blue contacts I still wore, and I blinked a few times fast, trying to clear the grit before I got too close to Mario again. I wanted to take them out, but I couldn't. Not without revealing my cards. But they'd been in for two days now, and I don't think they were meant to stay in this long.

I sighed heavily as I stirred cream into the coffee. *Not too much*, I reminded myself. Just a few drops. I didn't know what the point was, to be honest. Why not just drink it black? My mind wandered, seeking an escape from this reality, and it took some effort to bring it back to the task at hand. I hadn't slept since he'd brought me here. Even though I'd been thrown into a spare room, there was no lock on the door, and I'd spent the night sitting up in the corner of the bed watching the door, wondering how I should react when—not if—Mario decided to pay me a visit. Because I knew it was coming. He wouldn't leave me alone forever. But it seemed, for now at least, I'd been given a reprieve. He'd been in his office almost nonstop since we'd gotten here, and gave me the other bedroom so he wouldn't disturb me whenever he tried to get a few hours of sleep.

Exhausted as I was, I held the cup carefully with two hands as I walked barefoot across the large kitchen and set it in front of Luca's brother. He watched me closely, those dark eyes—so unlike the blue I was used to—not missing a thing.

"Thank you, baby," he said when I straightened. He sat at the head of the long table in his white button-down shirt and black slacks. Alone, except for me, after sending his men away. As per usual, I had no idea where we were. I'd spent the ride here lying on the floor in the back of a van, the sole of one of his men's dress shoes pressed against my neck to keep me there. But I did know we were in an apartment on the top floor of a five-story building on a quiet street. A suburb, maybe? I'd spent my first few hours listening for other people and watching out the window for cars coming or going, but there was nothing. No sounds. No cars. The rest of the building must be abandoned. It made sense. He wouldn't want anyone else in his business. But that also meant there was no one around who could possibly help me.

Backing away, I gave him a smile. "Anything else you want?" I thought maybe I should add an endearment to the end of that sentence, but I had no idea what my sister would've used. I wasn't normally around her boyfriends.

Mario's eyes ran over my face, then dropped to my breasts, nearly exposed as they were by the cut of the dress Luca had bought for me to wear. "Nah, honey, I'm good. Why don't you go wash your face? You remember where the bathroom is, right?"

His tone was innocent. But why would he ask me something like that? *Oh god. Oh god. He* is *just fucking with me.* "Of course. Don't be silly." I trailed my fingers over his shoulder as I walked away, heading toward the hall.

"Not that one," he said from behind me. "That one's not working. The other one."

Fuck.

Tossing him a shaky smile over my shoulder, I changed direction, keeping my steps slow and steady until I was out of eyesight. Desperately, I searched for a bathroom, finding one at the end of the hall at the back of the apartment. Switching on the light, I looked around the small room before shutting the door behind me and turning the lock.

Only then did I let myself breathe. Only then did I let the tears fall. Catching myself on the sink, I gave myself exactly thirty seconds to break down. I couldn't afford any more than that because if I stayed in here too long, he would come looking for me.

One of my contacts moved out of place and I shut that eye in fear of it falling down the sink. Turning on the faucet, I let the water run as I took it out and placed it in my palm. Carefully, I splashed some water into my hand and washed it off, then stuck it back into my eye. I did the same with the other one. I had no idea what this would do to my eyes, as I'd never worn contacts before in my life, but I couldn't stand the grit anymore. And I couldn't let Mario see my true eye color. If an eye infection saved my life, so be it. I just had to hang on until Luca came for me.

He *would* come for me, right?

Holy mother of god, I was so tired of the games these men were playing with my life. I just wanted to throw my cards down and walk out. But I couldn't. Not now. Not yet. For this particular challenge, the stakes were too high to fuck it up. Once again, my life was on the line.

I splashed some water on my face and then patted it dry with the white hand towel hanging on the gold holder. Honestly, a part of me just wanted to lose already. Give it up. Let one of them put a bullet through my head. At least then I wouldn't have to play anymore. But my survival instincts, honed by years of living in my sister's shadow, were too strong.

Deep down, I didn't just want to live.

I wanted to win.

CHAPTER 3
VEDA

I've been locked away in this fancy jail cell for two days now.

I think.

I pushed my dirty hair off my face and tried to remember. I was starting to lose track of time. Had it been longer? No, I don't think so. Lack of sleep and very little food was making my brain foggy, but I thought it had only been two nights. Which made today the second full day I'd been here, and I was still alive.

Closing my eyes for a moment, I let them tear up, hoping it would bring me some relief from these goddamned contacts. The fucking things burned like I'd washed them in nail polish remover, the whites of my eyes so red it made the blue stand out like they glowed.

How this idiot didn't know I wasn't Nicole was beyond me. He had to know. He *had* to. But if he did, he wasn't letting on, and it was totally messing with my head. Did he know, and he just got some kind of sick pleasure out of watching me skitter around this place trying to be her? Or was my sister such a mess that the way I was acting was normal behavior for her?

My nerves were so on edge, a scream lodged in my throat at every tiny noise. The scuff of a shoe. A cough. The click of a door closing. I felt like I was constantly on the verge of an epic freakout. There's no way he didn't notice how jumpy I was, and for the first twenty-four hours or so, I wondered why he didn't call me out. But then I realized he was distracted, and almost as jumpy as I was. And I knew what was happening.

We were waiting for Luca. It was quite obvious to me now that Mario had no intention of taking his hard fought for prize and escaping. No. He had no intention of running at all. He was using me as bait. Same as his fucking brother. And at this moment, I didn't know which one of them I hated more.

"Jesus, Mary, and Joseph, Nicole, go take a fucking shower already. I can't stand looking at you walking around here looking like some dirty, broken doll I picked up off the pavement."

Mario's angry voice broke into my thoughts. The comparison almost made me laugh, because wasn't that exactly what I was? However, I would literally kill for a shower right now. I was also terrified of being naked anywhere around this man. Game or not, I knew he would expect things from me. Things I tried not to think about because it made me want to vomit. He'd been so busy planning the execution of his brother, I was hoping he wouldn't notice that I was still running around in the same fancy dress I'd arrived in.

I glanced over at him, stuttering, "I wasn't sure if there was time..."

"Some of your clothes are in the closet in my room. Get a shower."

I sat frozen at the end of the couch. Mario and three of his men were in his office discussing business. They'd been in there all afternoon. He'd left the door open, and not knowing what else to do, I'd sat down and pulled a pillow into my lap until it was time to eat dinner. Luckily, I wasn't expected to cook. My sister had never made a meal in her life.

I stared at the piece of shit who had killed my sister. Bitch or not, she was still mine. My family. My twin. My eyes dropped to the gun holstered under his arm, and my fingers twitched. I wanted to feel the cold metal in my palm. Wanted to feel it kick as I shot a bullet into his head.

Mario narrowed his eyes and cocked his head. "Nicole. Go shower."

His tone was sharp. My eyes flew up to his face, then around at the others. I blinked, and the image of Mario bleeding out on the floor of his office dissipated. They all stared at me, waiting silently. "Um, okay. That'd be great. I feel super icky." Parroting one of my sister's favorite phrases, I could barely keep from rolling my eyes at myself. My body felt stiff and sore as I set the pillow aside and rose from the couch. My back ached from the tension I constantly carried around. With a small smile, I made my way down the hall, peeking back over my shoulder once.

Mario and his goons had closed the office door and were no longer watching me. As quickly as I could, I started opening doors, searching for Mario's room. The place we were in—although definitely high end—wasn't as large as Nicole's apartment, but it was big enough that it wasn't obvious where everything was. I found his room down another hall toward the back. It was the only door at this end of the apartment. When I opened it up, I knew right away it was his room. No one else here thought so much of themselves. I half expected to find King Henry VIII lounging on the plush red comforter of the raised bed. The area rug was red, too. The headboard and giant chest of drawers were black. Gold accents completed the look —an expensive vase, a box I assumed was for his watch or money clip or whatever, and a few other odds and ends. It was too gaudy, and I hated it. Nothing like the understated elegance of Luca's lake house.

I found the closet easily—almost as large as the guest room I was in—and stood staring around. A few things, my ass. Half the closet was filled with my sister's clothes and shoes, which, to be fair, was less than a quarter of her wardrobe. The other half contained Mario's suits, a few pairs of jeans folded over a hanger, and a shoe collection that rivaled my sister's.

He still had all of her things here. Why? Why not get rid of them? He'd killed her. He'd admitted it himself the night he took me from Luca. So…what? Was this some sick kind of mourning? Was he still hanging onto everything out of sentimental value?

Too tired to think more about it, I walked over to a chest of drawers on Nicole's side and opened the top drawer. Digging around, I found some scraps of silk and lace that were supposed to be underwear. The drawer beside it contained bras that matched. I grabbed the set that was made from the most material and closed the drawers.

Unfortunately, the rest of the selection wasn't much better. It was obvious that Nicole kept her comfy leggings and oversized T-shirts at her place. Her clothes here could best be described as "stripper wear"—everything tight and uncomfortable and not made to actually be worn for long. And being that I outweighed my sister by at least ten or fifteen pounds, this could prove to be an issue. I dug around and finally found a pair of black, stretchy pants with rhinestones down the side and a long-sleeved crop top with a low-cut neckline that matched the pants and looked like it would cover my boobs. It would have to do.

With clean clothes clutched in my hands, I left the closet. Halfway to the door, I stopped. Did Mario expect me to shower here, in his room? Frantically, I thought back to what he'd said, but there was nothing in my memory that told me anything one way or the other. Shit.

I took two steps toward the door and stopped, my heart pounding. The bathroom I was using was a shared room in the hallway. What was to stop any one of them from barging in there on me while I was naked with shampoo in my eyes? Maybe this wasn't a good idea.

But I *really* wanted to be clean. I felt like I'd been rolled around in that jar of used grease that my grandmother always saved and left sitting by the side of the stove, and I probably didn't smell much better. My eyes slowly crept across the room and landed on the open door to Mario's private bathroom. He'd been with his goons all afternoon. If I was quick, I could be in and out and dressed again, such as it was, before they finished their business.

Mind made up, I hurried across the room. The bathroom was done in all black and white and was just as obscenely large and overdone as the bedroom, but it was clean and it had a shower. A very large walk-in shower. But at least there was a wall surrounding it and not glass, so I had some semblance of privacy.

Moving fast now, I stripped off the dress I'd worn for Luca on our last night together. It seemed a lifetime ago now. My underthings came next. Putting a towel and my sister's clean clothes close to the shower, I walked in and turned on the water, letting it run until it was almost too hot to stand in. I wanted to soak in my demon water until I felt clean—not only of dirt, but of the fucked up things these men were putting me through.

There was a built-in shelf in the corner, and I removed the contacts and carefully set them in the back corner.

Honestly, the thought of putting those things back in my eyes made me want to cry. Maybe if I had some proper lense cleaner, or had even the slightest idea what I could use in place of it, they wouldn't be so bad. But as it was, I just didn't see how I could continue to wear them without risking my eyesight.

Maybe it was stupid of me to even try, anyway. As I tilted my head back to wet my hair, I wondered why I even bothered. How could Mario not know I wasn't my sister? He was engaged to her, a woman he should know inside and out by now.

But if he didn't, wouldn't he have called me out right away? Why play with me this way?

Except I thought I knew why. It was fun for him. Just like it was fun for Luca to kidnap me and keep me a prisoner in his house just so he could fuck with his brother and have his revenge, with no concern about me or my life. A surge of temper heated my blood to match the water as I dumped some shampoo on my head and began to work it through my long hair with jerky movements. I was fucking tired of being a pawn, and I wasn't going to do it anymore.

Before I could change my mind, I grabbed the contacts and squished them between my fingertips, then let the water wash them from my hand and down the large drain. There was a moment's panic when they didn't make it through the grate right away, but they disappeared before I could act on it.

And then they were gone.

The sound of my breath was loud over the soft spray of the water, my heart like thunder in my ears, and for a moment I couldn't move. But it was done. It was done. There was no turning back now. Shit. Mario would ask about my eyes. Or maybe he wouldn't. No, he would. And what the hell was I going to say?

Well, I'd just have to figure that out when I got there. For right now, I just wanted to get clean and get dressed before he finished his meeting and came looking for me. I found the body wash and wet the washcloth I'd brought into the shower with me, then covered it with soap and started scrubbing at my body. I'd just finished my face and arms and was working my way down my torso when I heard a click, like the sound of a door closing.

"Mind if I join you, baby?"

CHAPTER 4
VEDA

*N*o. No. No, no, no, no...

Chills skated across my skin despite the scalding hot water. Quickly, I started running the soapy washcloth over the rest of my body. "Oh, um. I was just about done. Give me just a sec and you can have the shower." Stupid, stupid, stupid! I never should've stayed in here. I should've taken my chances in the hall bathroom. I should've locked the fucking door. Should I not be in here? Should I apologize? "I just...you've been so busy... and I just..." My words stuttered out. Because what he said next answered that question, and made me realize it wouldn't have mattered where I'd chosen to shower.

"Why are you acting so weird? And since when do you know me as a man who prefers to shower alone? Although I've done it. Since you've been back, I've showered alone every fucking day. Slept alone. Trying to give you your space because I thought you might need a minute after living under my brother's roof, and with my hours being weird and shit..." He didn't finish his sentence. Instead, his hand landed on my hip and squeezed. "He fattened you up a bit for me. I like it. You've always been so fucking skinny."

The words, spoken directly behind me, so close his breath raised goosebumps on the back of my neck, iced the blood running through my veins. And when he touched me, bile rose in my throat until I thought I would gag.

I didn't say a word, but he went on talking, his soft palm running lazily up and down over my hip. So unlike the rough touch of Luca's hands, calloused from work and exercise. "I'm sorry I've neglected you these last few days. I've been very busy after my brother's...big reveal. But now that we've regrouped..." He made an appreciative noise, and I wondered how he could look at my naked body and not know the difference between me and my sister. A woman he was supposed to marry. "I'll have more time for us to get reacquainted."

"Yeah." My voice was breathless. Shaky. I cleared my throat, turning my face to the side so he could hear me. "Yeah, I know. It's okay. You don't haveta worry about me." No questions about what exactly I might have gone through as the prisoner of his brother. He'd never even asked me if I was okay. Just assumed I was mourning the absence of his dick this whole time. The Morelli men really needed a lesson in empathy.

I felt something poke my ass and barely resisted the urge to jump away. With our height difference, I knew exactly what it was, and could almost picture him standing behind me in my head, slightly shorter and stockier than his younger brother, the lines of his face a little deeper, eyes darker, hair a little grayer. But with the same nose. The same jaw. The same Mediterranean tone to his skin. His forearms were hairier than Luca's, his beard darker and thicker when it grew in, and the part of my brain that had removed itself from everything that was happening wondered if he'd also have more hair on other parts of his body, and my mouth twisted in disgust before I could stop it. Thank god I was facing away from him.

A moment later, my assumption was proven correct when thick arms wrapped around my waist from behind and a warm body pressed against my wet, naked back, his hard dick nestled in the crack of my ass. Mario's hands slid up my wet stomach to cup my breasts, squeezing them painfully before twisting my nipples between his fingers. The assault on my personal space was so sudden I stiffened automatically before remembering where I was and who exactly I was with. And what he could do to me if things went bad right at this moment. Closing my eyes, I forced myself to relax.

But my mind raced, trying to think of a way to get myself out of the shower pronto. I couldn't think with his hands running over my body with such familiarity. His dick pushed against my ass as one hand stayed on my breast and the other dipped between my legs, his fingers rough as they worked their way between the tender folds. I stiffened, inhaling sharply. Tears filled my eyes as I frantically tried to think. *Think, Veda! Dammit!*

"Mmmm," he moaned in my ear. "I've missed you, Nicole."

I forced my mouth to open, to say the words. "I've missed you, too."

"Yeah?"

"Yeah." One of his fingers hit my clit, his long fingernail cutting into the tender skin. It hurt, and without thinking, I grabbed his arm and tried to pull his hand away, but it was like trying to move a steel bar.

"You don't feel like you missed me," he murmured as he added another finger, forcing them up inside of me even though I lifted up onto my toes at the invasion. "As a matter of fact, you've been acting kinda shitty ever since I brought you here. Do you not appreciate what I fucking did for you? Huh?" His fingers tightened, hooking inside my body, his other hand digging into the soft flesh of my breast, and I knew I was going to have bruises the next day. "Risking my own fucking life for you? Answer me," he bit out, giving my entire body a small shake.

"Which part should I appreciate?" I asked. "The part where you shot me or the part where you got shot taking me back?"

He stilled behind me. "You know why I had to do what I did. You gave me no fucking choice, Nicole." He heaved a dramatic sigh. "Baby, you put my life in danger by blabbing my name on national television."

"I know," I told him. Somehow I kept my voice calm, level. "And I do appreciate you taking me away from your psycho brother. I just..."

"What?" he asked, his hands tightening possessively on my body. "You what? You want *him* now?"

"No. No, that's not what I was going to say."

Moving us forward with sudden force, he slammed me up against the tiles beneath the shower head, his arms taking the brunt of the hit. I raised both hands and pressed my palms to the cold ceramic, turning my face to the side just in time to avoid a broken nose. "What the fuck were you going to say, then?" He pressed his hips into my ass.

"I'm just...just..."

"Just what?" he gritted out. "Scared? Sorry?"

"I've just been through a lot," was my feeble explanation, but it was all I could think to say when the only thing I wanted to do was to get away from him.

"You fucked him, didn't you," he said slowly. "You fucked my own *fratello*." The word was said like a curse.

"No!" I hurried to deny, hoping he wouldn't hear the lie in my voice.. "No! That's not what I said." His rough hands still gripped my body, and I fought back a wince.

"You seem to be having a really hard time communicating today, Nicole."

"I know. I'm sorry. I'm tired," I told him. "I haven't been sleeping well."

His breath was hot on the back of my neck. "So explain yourself," he ordered.

"Just...it was hard, ya know? Your brother fucking kidnapped me, Mario. I was traumatized."

I felt him stiffen. "Did he hurt you?"

"Yes," I answered honestly. "He tried to strangle me once when I pissed him off." But that wasn't the most painful memory. No. The pain I remembered was the way my heart had split into a million pieces as Luca fucked me over the sink in the restroom of the club. The same club where he'd planned to murder me.

"Maybe you deserved it. You know you have a sassy mouth."

He wasn't lying about my sister. She did have a mouth on her that got her into trouble more often than not, but she also denied it with her last breath. "I didn't do anything. He was just in a bad mood."

"Well, now I'm in a bad mood," he told me. He suddenly released his hold on me, stepping back so fast I automatically tried to follow him, but I caught myself. "And you know what will make me feel better." Grabbing the tops of my arms, he spun me around. My wide eyes landed on his for a brief second before I remembered and dropped them, focusing on the healing wound in his right shoulder where Luca had shot him. It gave me a primal sense of satisfaction to see it. They had matching scars now.

I couldn't keep my real identity hidden forever. I knew that. But I'd really rather the big reveal didn't happen when we were naked in the shower together. My gut told me I wouldn't make it out of there the same woman I was when I'd entered, if I made it out at all.

But from the stillness of the man in front of me, I feared it was too late.

"Look at me," he ordered.

Trying to stay calm, I gathered the soapy washcloth to my chest and held it there, trying to preserve any sliver of modesty I had left. "Mario..."

"LOOK at me." His tone had an edge that hadn't been there before.

Fuck. Fuck. Fuck. Panic rose within me until my hands and feet were numb with it, my heart beating so fast and hard I saw stars in front of my eyes and wished I hadn't missed that last cardio appointment. Mario gripped my chin hard and forced my face up to his. The water from the shower sprayed the back of my head, smoothing down my wet hair and giving me nothing to hide behind. He stood in front of me without the grace of his younger brother, feet planted wide, blocking the entrance to the shower. I couldn't get around him. With nowhere to go and no way to stop what was about to happen, I opened my eyes, and held my breath as I waited to see how he would react.

He stared at my gray eyes for a long moment, and I knew what he was seeing. The color dull and murky compared to my sister's bright baby blues, although they already felt a hell of a lot better without the contacts irritating them. There was no emotion on his face as he studied the rest of my features, his eyes resting on my nose, my mouth, before finally letting go of my chin to step back so he could take a good look at the rest of me. Shoving my arms back down to my sides, he focused on the beauty mark near the nipple of my left breast, and I knew exactly what he was thinking. What he was remembering. My sister's breasts were flawless. His head tilted to the side. Slowly, he raised one hand, his fingertip sliding over the slightly raised, discolored bump with the softest of touches.

That simple touch scared me more than the violence I was expecting. By this point, my entire body was trembling so uncontrollably my muscles ached from it. I'd never been so afraid for my life before. Not even when Luca was pointing a gun straight at me.

"What the fuck is this?"

I watched him. Saw the moment it all started to click.

One side of his mouth lifted in a knowing smirk. "I have to admit, for a split second there, my brother had me fooled into thinking my big-mouthed fiancée had risen from the dead." His finger slid from the beauty mark to trace a path around my areola. He smiled when my nipple stiffened from the touch, despite my shudder of revulsion. "I thought, how the fuck could this be? I shot the bitch myself. Right in the fucking head. I mean, for a minute there, I thought I was seeing my first actual ghost." He paused, seeming to reflect back on the night in the parking lot. "Either that, or somehow the bitch had been way luckier than she deserved and she'd survived somehow. It's not like she'd miss the brain function the bullet took out."

My throat worked as I tried to force the words past my lips. "You...you really didn't know..."

His dark eyes rose to my face, the expression on his face coldly amused. But there was pain there, too. Pain and disappointment. "I wanted to believe you were her." He leaned in close to me, one hand wrapping around my throat and squeezing. Not hard enough to block the airflow, but just enough to let me know he could if he wanted to. Still, I dropped the washcloth to the tiles at my feet and wrapped my hands around his wrist. "But something was just...off, ya know? And even after I figured it out, there was still hope in my heart that my Nicole had somehow survived. And now that she knew to keep her fucking mouth shut, we could start over. Wanna know what ruined it for you?"

I managed a tiny nod.

"Because Nicole was never afraid of me. But not because she was brave." He shook his head. "No. You've got way bigger balls than she ever did. I can see that. It's because she was too fucking stupid. All that hair dye must've soaked into her brain or something. I don't know. But I knew, I knew it from the moment I got you back to this house and watched you walk around here like some poor little beaten bird, terrified to so much as look at me." All of this was said almost conversationally as he casually gripped my throat. "Nah, Nicole was never scared of me. She liked the danger. It was exciting to her. But you, you're smarter than your sister. And I assume you two were sisters. Twins, by how much you look like her. Am I right?"

I managed to nod again. The game was up. There was no use pretending anymore. "Funny she didn't mention me."

His brow furrowed. "You know, I think she might have. Once. Back when we were first dating. Of course, at the time, I was more interested in getting her out of the ridiculous outfit she was wearing. If for no other reason than that I just couldn't stand to look at it anymore. But after I found out that mouth of hers was good for something other than blabbering all the time, and I felt how tight her sweet pussy hugged my cock, eh"—he shrugged—"I decided I could deal with the outfits. Hell, her pussy was so good I was even willing to marry her so no other guy could have it. But I should've known it wouldn't last. She was too much of a public figure, and that big mouth of hers outed me the first chance she got. Told everyone I was back around." His expression turned dark, the chatty demeanor gone as fast as it had come. "You have the same mouth as your sister, and I bet it would look just as good wrapped around my cock."

No. No. No no no no...

CHAPTER 5
VEDA

With his hand still around my throat, he forced my head down with the other. "Get on your knees, bitch."

I resisted, shaking my head back and forth, and tried to keep my voice strong. "No. You don't want to do this. You're just hurting."

"So you're not so scared that you won't fight me, huh?" He shook the water out of his face. "Good. Fight. You've already got me so fucking hard I'm about to blow."

Even though I knew it would do no good, I did fight him, with one hand wrapped around his arm and the other trying to push him away from me as I tried to dislodge his grip on my throat. My feet slipped and slid on the tiles as I tried to stay standing, his large hand cutting off the air from my lungs. I tried to scream, but it came out garbled and weak. Mario laughed when he heard it.

Pushing down my panic, I forced myself to focus. To remember the things Enzo had taught me in our self-defense classes. Without warning, I let my feet slip out from beneath me and dropped, letting the weight of my body pull us both down, praying I wasn't about to smash the back of my skull against the tiles.

As I went down, the water sprayed me right in my face and I almost missed the comical look on Mario's as he lost his footing, throwing out his other hand in an effort to catch himself. His full weight landed on top of me, but I was prepared and used his surprise to twist the arm I was holding, forcing him to release his grip around my neck right before he crushed my windpipe. There was a crack above my head, and I hoped it was his forehead. Or his nose.

When everything stopped, I was lying on my back on the shower floor, the tiles warm and hard against my back and my face tucked into Mario's hairy armpit. I took stock of my body, but other than the overall feeling of being crushed by his heavier weight, it seemed like I survived with minimal bumps and bruises. But the respite was brief.

"You bitch! You fucking BITCH!"

My heart stopped completely, then began to pound fast and hard as Mario got up, his knee pressing painfully into my hip. I didn't follow him up, instead I flipped over onto my stomach as soon as his weight was off of me and pushed myself backward, the heel of one of his feet pulling the skin on my side as he barely avoided stepping on me. Blood ran like a river across the tiles and down the drain. I wasn't sure whose it was, and I wasn't about to hang around to find out.

If I wasn't so fucking terrified, this would be comical. Hysterical, even.

I scooched all the way out of the walk-in shower, not stopping until I felt the dry bathroom floor and saw my clothes and towel out of the corner of my eye. Grabbing the entire pile, I rose to my feet. I had no idea where I thought I was going, I just knew I had to get the hell out of there.

Mario's angry roar followed me as I got my footing and ran into his bedroom, naked as the day I was born, the towel gripped in one tight fist and my clothes in the other, my wet hair hanging in my face. I was halfway to the door when I was pulled up short by a wrenching pain on the back of my head. I screamed as my hair was ripped from my skull, dropping the towel as I grabbed his hand to try to save what hair I could. He let me go, and I was thrown onto the hard floor, twisting in midair. I landed with a grunt as pain shot from my hip and ricocheted down my thigh.

"You want me to hurt you? Is that it? You get off on that shit?"

"No." The word came out with a rush of air.

But he only chuckled as he wiped the blood from the gash on his forehead. "Oh, I think you do. Why else would you have pulled a stunt like that?" Naked as I was, his hard cock stuck out from its nest of curly dark hair and bobbed obscenely in front of his hips.

My nerves stretched taut, and fear made my stomach churn as I screamed, "To get away from you, you fucking psychopath!"

I knew the moment the words were out of my mouth that that was the wrong thing to say as the amusement faded from his eyes, replaced by a fury so cold that if I were a religious person, I'd be praying my ass off right now.

I tried a different tactic. "Mario, please. I'm not who you want. I'm not Nicole."

"I know you're not Nicole," he said. I watched in horror as he gripped his cock in his fist, pumping it a few times. "But Nicole isn't here. You are."

"But, but..." Frantically, I tried to think of something that would get through to him. "But you loved her. You were gonna marry her."

He smiled then, but it was mean and ugly. "I didn't love her. I loved to fuck her. And I loved the way she looked all dolled up on my arm."

He was lying. I could see in his eyes the way her death haunted him.

He shrugged as he stood over me, casually jacking off with blood running down his face and dripping off his chin. Drops landed on my stomach. "I loved that she was so desperate for a man, she let me do whatever I fucking wanted to her."

I didn't even want to know what that meant. But I could see the lines of pain around his eyes when he talked about her. I tried again. "You were going to marry her. That has to mean something." The words were barely louder than a whisper. And in a way, I felt betrayed for my sister. My mind couldn't wrap itself around the fact that she'd been willing to give up her life for this man. "She was an actress..."

"Yeah, that shit was gonna stop as soon as she said 'I do.' Too high profile. It was my mistake that I thought my secrets were safe—namely the fact that I was alive and well—until we tied the knot. How the fuck was I supposed to know she'd open her big mouth on TV? What the hell was that interview for anyway? She hadn't had any work in over a year." He seemed to almost forget me as he looked off into the distance, as though the answers to his questions were hidden somewhere in the wall. A few tense seconds ticked by, and then his attention snapped back to me, his eyes falling to his dick. He slid his hand faster up and down the length. "Ah, fuck...you're making me lose my hard on."

A flood of relief made me lightheaded, and I sat up with a wince, pain shooting from my hip as I pulled the towel around me, hoping he would let me go back to my room. I felt, more than saw, when my movements grabbed his attention again.

"Where do you think you're going, *Nicole?*" He dragged my sister's name out.

I froze and stared at the floor in front of me. I didn't bother to respond. It wouldn't do any good. He was going to do with me what he would. I felt helpless. And so alone.

"Get on your knees and put your mouth on my cock."

I tried one last time to ring some sympathy from him. "Mario, please."

His upper lip curled in disgust at my pleas. "On. Your. Fucking. Knees."

My mind raced, but I couldn't think of anything Enzo had taught me that would apply to this situation. I couldn't kick him; he was in the wrong spot, standing near my injured hip, so all I would have to do is get up onto my knees and turn my head to put him in my mouth. I could grab him around the ankle and try to pull his leg out from underneath him, but I didn't know if I had the strength.

Before I could figure out some way to get away from him, he gripped me by my hair again, the wet strands making it easy for him to lift me up until I knelt before him, and his limp dick was at face level. "Suck it," he ordered. "And you'd better make it fucking good after all the shit you just pulled." He prodded my lips with the tip, his breaths growing heavy as his dick began to thicken. "Cuz if you don't, I'll really have no reason to keep you around."

Bile rose in my throat, and I clamped my jaw closed, refusing to take him into my mouth.

"Bitch, you better open that sweet mouth."

I glared up at him, letting every ounce of hatred show in my eyes. His narrowed as he read my expression. "Don't even fucking think about it. Or I'll put a bullet in your fucking head right now, just like I did with your sister, then dump your body on my brother's doorstep."

Luca.

The filth Mario continued to spew was drowned out by the roaring in my ears as something icy cold stirred inside of me at the thought of his brother. My hands shook with rage, and I clenched them into fists at my sides. At this moment, I hated him. I hated him with everything in me. For taking me from my normal, boring life. For putting me into this situation. For being such a bastard and making me fall for him anyway. So much so I'd stood there willing to let him shoot me for his petty revenge.

Mario jerked my head up, his grip on my hair so tight I could feel more strands ripping from my skull. "Open your fucking mouth, or I'll call my boys in here and have them hold you down while I knock out your fucking teeth and shove my dick so far down your throat, I'll be able to feel you swallow."

I unclenched my jaw, a sound of hatred and disgust erupting from me as he pushed his cock between my lips. The urge to bite him was strong. To sink my teeth so deep I tasted blood.

"Wider," he ordered as he pushed the head against my teeth.

I held my towel in a death grip over my bare chest with one hand and pushed against his thick thigh with the other, trying to keep him from going too deep. But it didn't do any good. As soon as I let him in, he shoved his cock to the back of my throat until I gagged, my eyes filling with tears that spilled over and ran down my face. I was on the verge of puking all over him when he finally pulled back, but I only had time to suck in a quick breath before he was shoving it back into my mouth. I tasted the bitter tang of come leaking from the head onto the back of my tongue and was never so glad that I had nothing in my stomach as I began to heave uncontrollably.

It didn't move him. If anything, my disgust excited him more. His breaths were loud and harsh above me as he grabbed my head in both hands and started fucking my mouth fast and hard. Tears ran down my face as I struggled to breathe, my mind dissociating itself from what was happening, like I was watching this happen to somebody else. Some different girl.

As he pulled out and came all over my face and chest, I just kept thinking to myself that it could be so much worse than a forced blow job. At least I was still here. And I was still alive.

But this was only the beginning of what he had planned for me.

CHAPTER 6
LUCA

Veda had been gone for five days, and I was losing my fucking mind holed up in this house "for my own safety." Nothing helped. Not drinking. Not working. Not even beating the fuck out of the bag in my gym, like I was doing now, until my knuckles were bloody and bruised and I could barely stay standing.

My phone vibrated where I'd left it on top of the small fridge. I almost didn't hear it as I pounded the bag, and when I did, I seriously considered not answering it. But maybe it wasn't my father calling to berate me some more. Maybe it was news.

I grabbed my towel and wiped my face and chest as I strode across the room and picked it up. The number was private. My gut clenched with foreboding, and I tapped the green phone button, lifting it to my ear. I didn't say anything, just listened as I fought to catch my breath.

"Hello, brother."

The sound of his voice caused a flash of red-hot rage to rush through my bloodstream so fast it made me lightheaded. I gripped the phone hard, surprised it didn't crack apart, but then the fog cleared away just as fast as it had hit and my focus became razor sharp.

The son of a bitch better not have harmed a single hair on her head. I forced myself to sound calm. Unconcerned. He already knew I couldn't end the game the way I had planned. I needed to play this off. If he knew exactly what she meant to me, how it fucked me up inside that he had her, there was no way she would survive this. "What do you want, Mario?"

"I thought you might be interested to know that your little game piece here is still alive and well. But I can't promise you how long she's gonna stay that way."

I grabbed a water from the fridge and took a long swallow, purposefully making him wait. "And why would you think I care? You won. Again. It's over."

"Ah, come on now, Luca. I saw your face when you were pointing that gun at her. Heard the way she spoke to you. You really think I don't know what's between you two?"

I had to play this oh so carefully. "So, I fucked her. And I decided her cunt was worth more to me than your life, so I shot you instead. Not because I feel anything for her, but because I care so little about you. Was there something else you wanted? I'm in the middle of a workout."

That threw him off for a second. Then I heard a scuffle on the other end of the line, and I heard Veda cry out.

Breathe. In. Out. In. Out. Slow and steady.

"So you wouldn't care if I put a bullet through this imposter's eye?"

I wasn't surprised that he knew who Veda really was. I never expected him to be so stupid that he wouldn't figure it out real quick. I knew I would have only a few seconds to pull everything off without him realizing she wasn't his fiancée brought back to life.

And I'd paused. Everything that happened afterwards was on me. My fault. But I wasn't going to have her death on my conscious. I *would* get her back. But I wasn't going to walk into his trap to do it. "Do what you want. I really don't give a fuck." I held the phone away from my ear and stared at the screen for a moment, gritting my teeth as I fought the urge to reassure her. Then I tapped the screen and ended the call.

As soon as the screen went black, I ran out of the room and headed to my office. Enzo was already there when I arrived. "Anything?"

Something dull and heavy crushed my insides when he shook his head. "No. I'm sorry. We couldn't get a trace on it."

I threw the phone to the floor, where it bounced once and hit the leg of one of the chairs that sat in front of my desk. "Fuck!" Hands in my hair, I began to pace back and forth, my bare feet silent on the hard floor. "What have I done? What the fuck have I done?"

"He won't kill her," Enzo reassured me. "He'd only kill her if he thought you gave a shit about her. I was listening in on the call. You were completely convincing."

I didn't believe him. "No. He's going to kill her. She's no use to him now."

"He won't. Remember, I know him almost as well as I know you. He won't be convinced. He'll try to think of a way to use her to get to you. His first plan didn't work. He's going to move on to plan B."

I stopped in the middle of the room, my eyes on the floor. Enzo was right. Mario wouldn't give up this easily. If nothing else, he was tenacious. Like a dog with a bone when he thought he had something.

He had to be fucking right.

"Luca, you need to get some sleep."

I ignored Tristan's well-meaning advice as I had been for the past three days since I'd gotten Mario's phone call. Along with Enzo's nagging. How the fuck did they expect me to sleep when she was with my brother? The same guy who'd put a bullet through the last woman I cared about without one ounce of remorse. And I didn't know if she was alive or dead or...

Something far worse.

Enzo and Tristan believed I'd played it off well. But I knew my brother. And worse, he knew me. He knew that in the short time she'd been here, Veda had managed to worm her way under my skin, burrow through the bone and muscle, and forge her way through the impenetrable wall around my heart.

He knew. He had to know.

"Are you sure you don't want to ask Luigi for help with this?"

My temper flared before I could control it and I had to take a few deep breaths so I didn't snap at one of the few true friends I had. My father was the last person on this fucked up earth I wanted to turn to for help. It was a testament to the friendship Tristan and I shared that I managed to keep the volume of my voice level. "No. I'll handle this myself. This is between me and Mario. My father has made it clear he's not getting involved, even if I wanted him to. He won't choose between his sons." The mafia boss apparently did have a weakness after all. After all these years of him lecturing me about how disgusted he was by my own, he wasn't such a hard ass himself. Not when it came to his family. However, he'd also made it very clear he wouldn't interfere, as long as I kept Mario alive.

That was going to be hard to do this time around.

"Look. I'm here for you, Luca. What do you need me to do?"

I stared into the amber liquid that filled the glass in my hand and felt my mouth twist with fury. "I needed you to fucking protect her, that's what I needed you to do."

He was smart enough not to respond this time. I mean, it was a stupid thing to say. I'd taken Veda to that club so I could put a bullet through her head in front of my brother. Just like he'd done to Maria, the woman I'd loved years ago. Accusing Tristan of such a thing was ridiculous. But I needed to lash out at someone. And he was in the room.

I downed what was in my glass and immediately refilled it from the bottle of whiskey on my desk.

"I'm going to go find Enzo and see if he had any luck talking to his contacts."

"Yeah," I told him without looking at him. "You do that."

Tristan got to the door and stopped. He didn't turn around, but only turned his head enough that I could hear him. "You know I would protect Veda with my life, even from you, if you'd only given the word. Not because I give a rat's ass about her. But because I do give a shit about you."

I glanced up at him. Tristan's large form filled the doorway, and I could tell by the tense hold of his shoulders that I'd hurt him with my careless words. "Fuck," I mumbled. Then I took a deep breath. "I apologize," I told him sincerely. "I'm just..." Scared. Hurt. Angry. Ashamed. "...tired."

He nodded once and went to find Enzo.

"Fuck. Fuck!" Slamming my empty glass down on my desk, I dropped my head into my hands. What the fuck was wrong with me? Making an enemy of Tristan wasn't a good idea right now. I needed him on my side. Always. If anyone else had mouthed off to him the way I just had, he would've taken out the window behind me with their airborne body.

Luckily, he'd known me long enough to know how I am. He also knew I was one of the few people who could match him in a fight. He accepted my authority only because he had no interest in it himself. Not that that was an excuse to accuse him of not having my back. I knew how lucky I was to have his loyalty. I was only one of two people in the world who did. Enzo being the other. And I almost felt bad for the fuckers who didn't.

Almost.

Disgusted with myself, I got to my feet. The room spun around me, and I had to acknowledge that he was right. I was drunk, and I'd barely slept since Mario had taken Veda. I had all of my best guys on the hunt for her, but so far, there hadn't been one single hint of where he could possibly have taken her. But I would find her eventually. And when I did, I couldn't be strung out on whiskey and going on an hour of sleep a night. I needed to be sharp. And I needed to be ready to fight my way out of there with her if need be.

Moving slowly, I left my desk and made my way upstairs to my bedroom. As I passed by the kitchen, I heard water running and the click of the gas stove, which meant Lisa was already in there getting her tea before she prepared dinner. Enzo and Tristan sat at the far side of the room in the chairs near the patio doors that led out to the back deck and the pool. Both of them had their phones to their ears. Tristan glanced up as I passed, saw I was headed toward the stairs, and went back to his conversation.

Even with other people in the house, it felt cold and empty without Veda's raw energy filling it. She warmed it better than the hot Texas sun. Made it into a home. A home I never realized I was lacking until she came into my life.

A surge of frustration made my head pound. She would warm this house again. If I had to lock her inside for the rest of her life to keep her here, I would. I had no doubt she hated me after everything I'd put her through. But her hate was better than this constant chill in my bones. This constant ache in my chest.

When I got upstairs to my room, I paused in the doorway. Without conscious thought, my head swiveled toward the room Veda had chosen for her own. Before I knew what I was doing, my feet took me down the hall.

As soon as I opened the door, her scent hit me full in the face, forcing a groan of longing that started somewhere within the hole in my chest and pushed its way up and out of my parted lips. I closed my eyes and inhaled her into my lungs, holding her there like a hit from a joint, craving the high only she could give me.

I wouldn't allow Lisa to come in and clean or change anything since Veda had last used this room. The bed was still unmade. Her clothes were still lying in the chair where she'd thrown them. The closet door was wide open, the items inside split between what she liked to wear on one side and what her sister would wear on the other. The clothes I'd forced her to buy. Forced her to wear. The person I'd forced her to become.

My feet moved until I stood at the foot of the bed, the door softly clicking shut behind me. I stared at the blue comforter, still rumpled from the last time she'd slept here. The night I took her to the club. I'd allowed her to stay in here in an effort to put some distance between us. To get her out of my blood. It didn't work. I still remembered how soft her skin was as it slid against mine. The smell of her. The taste of her.

Unbuttoning the top three buttons of my dress shirt, I reached over my head and pulled it the rest of the way off, leaving me bare chested. I kicked off my shoes and dropped my black jeans and boxer briefs to the floor to join them. Naked, I crawled up into her bed and yanked the comforter up over my head until I was surrounded with Veda's scent. I inhaled and exhaled slowly. Once. Twice.

My hand found my cock, already half hard. Closing my eyes, I let myself remember...

Veda lying beneath me that first night, my blade pressed into her cheek. The taste of her blood on my tongue.

Veda sprawled face down across my lap, her sweet ass pink from the palm of my hand.

Veda straddling my lap with my cock deep inside of her, her head thrown back with abandon, her gorgeous breasts filling my hands like they were fucking made for me and me alone.

Her gray eyes filled with defiance. The way she would kiss me with all of that passion locked up inside of her. Her sweet ass in the air as I pounded into her pussy.

Pleasure shot down my spine and concentrated in my balls. I could practically taste her pussy on my tongue, hear her moans in my ears, feel the way she hung on to me when she was about to come like I was the only thing keeping her on this earth...

"Ahhh!" I came hard, rolling to the side as my come shot out in spurts, coating the sheets beside me. Afterward, I laid there in a daze as I caught my breath. Exhausted, my scent mingling with hers under the warmth of the comforter, I closed my eyes and finally fell into a dreamless sleep.

Some time later, Enzo found me there. My eyes shot open as soon as I felt his hand on my shoulder. I blinked against the light coming in from the hall. "What is it?" My voice was gravely with sleep and my mouth tasted like something had died in there.

"We found her."

CHAPTER 7

LUCA

For a moment, I couldn't move. But then I burst from the bed in a flurry of movement. Enzo quickly stepped back out of the way, not in the least concerned about my nakedness. "Where is she?" I asked him. I wanted to ask him if she was alive, but I couldn't bring myself to say the words.

"At Lisa's."

I froze with my hands on the button of my jeans. "What?"

"She's at Lisa's. Woke them up banging on the door after she found her way to their house. Apparently, she was dumped near there."

Found their house. That meant she was up and walking on her own. "He just left her there?" It wasn't lost on me that my brother had found the home of one of my most trusted employees. "Who dropped her off? Did they see anything?"

He shook his head. "No."

I picked up my shirt from the floor, unable to look at him as I asked my next question. "Is she all right?"

"I just know she's alive and walking and talking."

That's all I could really ask for. So why was my gut clenched with the need to see her? Hear her voice? Enzo on my heels, I rushed down the hall to my own room, carrying my shoes. "Call for the car. And call Lisa. Tell her and her husband to pack their things. They're coming here. Just what they can fit in the car for right now. We'll get the rest of their stuff later." Enzo was already on his phone, barking out instructions. "Actually, make it two cars. I want one of you with me and Veda, and one with Lisa and her husband."

"I'm on it."

He left me at my bedroom door, striding down the hall to the stairs to carry out my orders while I ran inside to brush my teeth and change. Five minutes later, I was heading downstairs in a clean, black T-shirt and jeans, my gun in its shoulder holster. I didn't bother with a jacket. I didn't want anything to get in the way if I needed to use it. When I got outside, Enzo and Tristan were waiting beside the first SUV, dressed similarly to me. Two of my best drivers were behind the wheels in case we got into a situation. As I rushed up to the first car, Tristan opened the back door for me.

"Let's go." They both climbed in with me and ten seconds later, we were on our way. No one spoke. There was no need. We'd been in situations like this enough times to know what needed to be done.

Lisa's house was forty-five minutes from mine, with traffic. However, it was still dark, and the roads were relatively empty, so we made record time. Still, they were the slowest fucking twenty minutes of my life. For the fifth time, I rubbed my sweaty palms up and down my jean clad thighs, my eyes out the window, watching for anyone who was following us.

"You okay, Luca?" Enzo asked from the passenger seat.

"Fine."

He gave me a nod and turned back to face the front.

"We could be walking into a trap," Tristan said quietly from beside me.

"I have no doubt," I told him.

"How do you want to handle this?"

"Drop Tristan off a block away," I told my man behind the wheel. "Don't stop. Just slow down enough around the corner so he can jump out."

"Yes, sir."

Without another word, Tristan drew his weapon and checked it.

"Let me know what you find."

One hand on the door handle and his eyes watching out the window, he gave me a nod.

"Here we go," Enzo said.

The car slowed to take a sharp curve and Tristan opened the door and jumped out. Leaning over, I pulled it shut again as the car sped up. Tristan would cut across the empty property around Lisa's on foot, arriving at the house before we did. If anyone besides Lisa and her husband were there waiting for us, we would know well in advance.

Many would think I was a fool to only send in one man, but they didn't know Tristan.

When we arrived at Lisa's small home on the outskirts of Jonestown, I wasn't surprised to find Tristan standing at the dead end of the road, just before it turned into dirt and curved off into the trees. We had about an hour before sunrise, if the glow in the sky was any indication. I scanned the trees surrounding us as the SUVs pulled off the road in front of the house, still not convinced I wasn't going to be shot the moment I left the vehicle. Lisa's car and her husband's truck were parked in the driveway, and there were lights on inside the house. Nothing else stirred. "Leave the engine running," I told my driver.

Tristan came around to my side and opened my door. "It's all clear."

I made no move to get out. "You're sure?"

"I searched the grounds. There's one set of tire tracks that shows whoever dropped her off turned around there"—he pointed to the beginning of the dirt road—"and left. No one else is around. I made sure of it."

Then why did my gut still tell me this was a setup?

Enzo got out of the passenger side and headed toward the house, one hand on his gun and his eyes scanning the area all the way to the front door. When he got there, he didn't immediately knock or go in. Instead, he put his back to the door, scanned the area one more time, then gave me the signal that it was safe for me to get out. Tristan walked with me, watching my back.

When I reached Enzo, he moved out of the way, the two of them acting as human shields behind me, just in case. But it was eerily quiet as I opened the door and went inside. "Veda? Lisa?"

"In here!" Lisa called from the kitchen.

I pulled my gun and kept it in front of me as I carefully made my way along the edge of the living room until I came to the archway that led into the kitchen. "Lisa?"

She walked over to the archway to meet me. She was wrapped in a soft-looking pink and gray robe, her hair sticking out all over her head, but her eyes were calm and steady, and her posture relaxed. "She's in here," she told me. "I made her some tea."

Ah. Tea. Lisa's magic cure all.

Holstering my weapon, I hurried into the kitchen.

Veda was sitting at the table, her hands wrapped around a steaming mug. All I could do was stare at her. She had a bruise on her jaw and a haunted look in her eyes when she raised them to mine. "Are you hurt?"

"Define 'hurt,," she said.

"Physically. Are you hurt physically?"

She looked up at me then, and there was no life in her eyes. "Nothing that won't heal."

"Veda—"

But she held up her hand and cut me off. "Don't. Just... don't."

I took a breath. She was here. And she was alive. That's all I fucking cared about right now. I turned to Lisa. "Did Enzo get through to you?"

"Yes. Kevin is in the bedroom packing some bags. I just need to get dressed. I didn't want to leave Veda alone."

"Thank you," I told her. "Go do that and bring your things out. I'll stay with her."

My eyebrows rose in surprise when Lisa turned to Veda and asked, "Is that okay?"

She nodded, and Lisa patted her shoulder and went to do as I'd told her, shooting me a warning look on her way out.

I watched her go, half amused and half annoyed at that little performance.

"So what are your plans for me now?" Veda's voice was dull. Lifeless. Like her eyes.

"I just want to take you home."

A small spark of hope was there and gone in a flash. "I don't suppose you're talking about my home?"

"I'm talking about the lake house. Where you'll be safe."

"Safe from who, exactly?"

"Veda..." I trailed off, not knowing what to say.

Taking a last sip of her tea, she rose from the table and walked stiffly over to the sink, where she rinsed out her cup. I watched her closely, searching for any sign that she was injured, despite her assurance otherwise. She was wearing tight black leggings and a leopard print blouse that was too tight across her breasts. My cock stirred as I noticed the buttons straining to hold it together. She had something black and lacy underneath.

"These are my sister's clothes," she told me. "His closet was half full of them."

I nodded. I wanted to close the distance between us and take her into my arms so I could hold her close and feel the warmth of her body, feel the way her curves fit against me so perfectly, but she stood so stiff and still, and I knew she didn't want me touching her. It made me angry. A stupid reaction. But it seemed that's all I was capable of these days. "Did you bring anything with you?"

She shook her head. "No."

"Let's get out of here, then."

She didn't try to argue with me, just gave a resigned sigh and walked out of the room, giving me a wide berth. I reminded myself she was allowed to feel the way she did. I mean, what the hell did I expect? That she would run into my arms? Profess her undying devotion to me?

No, I deserved the way she was treating me. I deserved her hatred. Her disgust. Her distance.

But I didn't accept it.

Following her out to the SUV, there was a bit of a delay when Veda didn't want to ride with me until I physically picked her up and put her in the vehicle after I ordered her inside and she refused. But despite the trouble she gave me, my heart soared, happy to see she hadn't completely lost her spirit. I could handle her when she fought with me; that only told me she still felt something. It was when she stopped fighting that I got worried.

Once Lisa and her husband, Kevin, were loaded up into the SUV behind us, we headed back to the lake house, taking a roundabout route to make sure we weren't being followed. Once we arrived, I sent the guys up to one of the spare bedrooms with their things.

"Oh, Mr. Morelli, you don't have to do that," Lisa insisted. "We can stay out in the guest house, if Tristan doesn't mind."

"I insist," I told her. "I know it's not ideal for your privacy, but I want you both in the main house where it's safe. Just in case."

Lisa's eyes filled with tears. "Thank you."

I gave her a nod, uncomfortable with her gratitude. "Of course. You're a part of the family. And I have plenty of room."

As she and her husband followed their things upstairs to one of the spare rooms, I felt Veda's eyes on me. "What?" I asked her.

She stared at me a moment longer. "I'm just trying to figure out how you can be such a decent man and yet such a fucking bastard all at the same time."

"It's a natural talent."

"Obviously."

We stood at an impasse, our eyes on each other. Both wary, but for completely different reasons. Unable to stand the silence anymore, I asked her if she'd like to go take a shower and change. "All of your things are still in your room. Just as you left it."

Without another word, she left me standing there by the front door. I watched her walk slowly up the stairs, wishing she would allow me to help her. She looked beyond exhausted. But I knew I wouldn't be welcome, so I headed to my office and the empty glass I'd left on my desk that desperately called to be filled.

CHAPTER 8
VEDA

He wasn't lying. My room was exactly as I'd left it, all the way down to the crumpled blankets on the bed and my sneakers kicked off in the corner.

Grateful to be alone, I took a deep breath and froze. It smelled like Luca in here. Had he been creeping around in my room while I was gone? Looking for what? Too tired to think about it, I just shook my head and went to the closet to find something to sleep in. The sun was coming up, but I was so fucking tired. I needed to sleep. And strangely enough, I felt safe here.

As I pulled off my dead sister's clothes and left them lying in a heap on the bathroom floor, I had to wonder, what was he planning to do with me now? The game was up. Mario knew who I was. Or rather, who I wasn't. And Luca hadn't so much as asked me to close my eyes when we drove to his house, which meant I knew the location of the house now. His private sanctuary that, by his own words, not even his own family knew about.

What the hell did that mean?

Turning on the shower, I gave it a minute to warm up before stepping beneath the spray. A hiss of pain escaped me when the water ran over my body, but I refused to look down to see the reason why. Wouldn't watch as the water ran bloody down the drain.

For a while I just stood there, letting the shower beat down on the back of my neck, my eyes squeezed shut, as much to hold back the tears as so I wouldn't see. I was so done with all of this. I just wanted to walk out the door and go back to my boring, lonely life. Forget everything that had happened.

But even as I longed for the life that had been torn out from under me, a part of me rebelled against the idea. Ached at the very thought. I was too tired to analyze it. And too tired to deny it. So what I did was ignore it as I washed my hair and body, turned off the shower, and reached for the towel on the rack, carefully keeping my emotions in check because I was afraid that once I set them free, I would never recover.

For the second time since I'd come in here, I froze. Someone was in my room. I could hear them moving around. I walked over to the partially open door and listened. Whoever it was, it sounded like they were making my bed.

Assuming it was Lisa, I closed the door and finished drying off before I pulled on my sleep shorts and the T-shirt with the multicolored peace signs all over it. I loved this set. It saddened me that my blood might ruin it. With that in mind, I started opening the cabinet doors, looking for something I could use as a bandage. I found a first aid kit under the sink and took out the gauze bandages and some medical tape.

It was hard to cover things up without looking in the mirror, but I just went by the way it burned and hoped the bandage was large enough. When I was finished, I hid the wrappers back in the first aid kit and put it back under the sink.

When I opened the door, I was surprised to find Luca in there, smoothing down a clean top sheet on my bed. "What are you doing?"

He glanced up, his eyes traveling from the top of my head to my bare feet, then stood and picked up the comforter from the floor. "I wanted you to have a clean bed to sleep in."

"Have you been sleeping in here?"

If my question caught him off guard, he didn't show it. Walking around the bed, he pulled the comforter up over the pillows and evened it out over the side of the mattress. "I did last night."

"Why?"

Finished with what he was doing, he straightened and looked me right in the eye. "Because I missed you."

"You missed me?" I barely bit back a laugh.

"I did. I was worried about you, Veda."

Holy shit. The gall of this guy. "Are you fucking kidding me right now?" I asked him. "You were going to *shoot* me, Luca."

"I didn't shoot you."

My exhausted brain tried to keep up with what he was saying. Was he trying to tell me that he never planned to shoot me at all? But no, that wasn't true. He was. I'd felt it all the way down to my bones both that night, and now. And would it matter either way? Really? This guy had done nothing but fuck with me since the moment he laid eyes on me. "But you *were* going to shoot me."

He was quiet for a long time. "Yes," he finally said.

Yes.

His expression was completely impassive. I couldn't read him. And honestly, I didn't want to try. I just wanted to sleep. Maybe forever. "Please get out of my room. I can't talk to you right now. I just want to sleep." Walking over to the bed, I pulled back the clean blankets and climbed in.

"Veda, we need to talk."

"Luca, please. I'm so fucking tired."

After a moment, he said, "Okay."

I heard something rustling behind me and assumed he was picking up the dirty sheets. So I was surprised when a gust of cool air hit my back right before his warm body curled around mine, his muscular arm sliding around my waist and holding me there when I stiffened and tried to pull away. "What the fuck are you doing?"

"You can sleep with me here, or you cannot sleep at all and we can talk. Either way, I'm not fucking leaving your side right now." He was quiet a moment, and then, "I *can't* leave your side right now."

Jesus Christ. Was this guy for real? After everything I'd been through the last week, I didn't think it would be possible, but eventually, I started to relax against him. My eyes slid closed, and my mind shut down as sleep started to pull me under.

Luca slid his hand beneath my tee, moaning when he laid it flat on the bare skin of my stomach. I tried to stay awake, fully expecting him to try to fuck me. And I couldn't let him do that, even if I wanted to. I couldn't let him see. But he didn't try anything. And eventually, his even breathing lulled me into unconsciousness. So I wasn't sure if it was real or not when I heard him whisper, "I'm never letting you go again, my *vita*. My life."

I CAME BACK to full consciousness slowly, like I was swimming up from the deep end of the pool. I bobbed on the surface of the water for a moment, only to sink back into the peaceful depths. Someone tucked the comforter close around me, and then I fell back into oblivion.

The second time, I became aware of birds chirping outside and I smiled. But I fell asleep again without realizing it.

It wasn't until the third time that I was able to stay awake. Mostly because of the pressure of my bladder.

Opening my eyes, I blinked against the sunlight and immediately closed them again with a moan. Who the hell opened the blinds? Or maybe they just burned so much still because of the damage done by the contacts. Gradually, I was able to keep them open, and I noticed the sun was nearly in the same position it was in when I went to sleep.

Please tell me I'd slept more than an hour.

Was Luca still asleep? Afraid of waking him, I carefully turned my head to look over my shoulder.

He wasn't in the bed.

With a sigh of relief, I flopped over onto my back, wincing as the wound on my chest pulled. Or maybe it was the tape. Good god, I had to pee. My hand crept up over my shirt, probing at the bandage that was pulling.

"Good morning. I was starting to worry you weren't ever going to wake up."

My head snapped to the side, and my arm flopped back down to the bed. Luca was sitting in the chair in the corner of my room, looking freshly showered and shaved and dressed in his usual attire of black slacks and a black button-down shirt. He had what I had dubbed his "house shoes" on his feet, a pair of black loafers.

"You've been asleep for over twenty-four hours," he told me. His eyes dropped to the bruise on my jaw and then lower, where I'd been touching my chest. "How are you feeling?"

"Like I have to pee," I said, as I jumped out of bed and rushed to the bathroom. I took my time, brushing my teeth and running a brush through my tangled hair, then braiding it into a single, loose French braid that hung down to the middle of my back. I didn't help. I felt no more human than when I'd come in here, but at least my bladder was empty. Knowing I couldn't hide in there forever, I braced myself and opened the door.

Luca was sitting exactly where I'd left him, his elbows on his knees with his fingers laced and his head hanging forward. When he heard me come out, he looked up, his blue eyes traveling from the top of my head to my bare feet and back again, only slower on the way back up.

"So, what now?" I blurted. "What happens now?"

Moving slowly, Luca stood, sliding his hands into the front pockets of his slacks. He just looked at me for a long time.

"What happens now, Luca?" Surprisingly, I felt quite calm as I waited for him to tell me what my future would behold. Or if I'd have a future at all.

"You stay here with me," he finally said.

"For how long?"

He ignored my question. "You can stay in this room if you're comfortable here."

"Alone?"

"Not alone," he told me in that same neutral tone.

"You're going to force me to sleep with you every night?"

"Yes," he said without hesitation.

I eyed him. Though his posture was relaxed, there was a steel glint in his blue eyes and a set to his jaw that told me arguing with him would do no good. But still, I tried. "What if I don't want you in here?"

"I don't care."

I crossed my arms over my chest, then dropped them again when it hurt. "So after everything you put me through, you're telling me that after all that *shit*, what I want doesn't matter? Like at all."

His eyes traveled over my face. I couldn't read what was there. "I have some things to take care of," he told me as he walked out of the room. "I just wanted to be here when you woke up." And with that, he left me alone in my prison.

After he'd gone, I stood there for a long time, unsure of what to do with myself. Memories of my days with Mario crashed through me, no longer held off by exhaustion and force of will. I swayed where I stood, the room spinning around me until I realized I wasn't breathing. My mouth gaped open like a fish out of water, and I stumbled over to the bed, sat down, and put my head my head between my knees until the feeling passed and I could drag in a shaky breath. I stayed like that, just breathing, until the panic attack or whatever the hell that was had passed.

I sat up and rubbed my face with my hands. "I'm okay. I'm okay. I'm not there anymore. I'm here. I'm here."

Luca's words came back to me. I wouldn't be alone. He would be here with me every night, whether I wanted him here or not. A sense of comfort draped over me like a soft blanket. Looking around the room, I finally recognized what it was I was feeling.

Relief.

CHAPTER 9
LUCA

"Luca, can I talk to you for a sec?"

Tristan was waiting for Enzo and me when I got out of the SUV. I was just getting home from my newest club, I was tired and hungry, and I wasn't really in the mood for whatever the hell it was that made Tristan have that look on his face. Some shit had gone down between one of my guys and a member of the cartel who was in town to make a collection from me. The bartender called me as soon as things started to get heated, and I'd gotten there just in time to keep my cousin from getting shot. I didn't need this shit right now. I had other things to worry about here at home.

"Can it wait?"

"No. I don't think it can." He and Enzo exchanged a look I couldn't quite read.

My stomach growled. I was anxious to get inside to see if I could coax Veda into having dinner with me. "Can we at least go in the house?"

Tristan put a hand on my arm as I went to walk past. "Luca, just give me a minute here."

I stopped, glancing back at him over my shoulder. Something was seriously bothering him. "Okay." Putting my empty stomach out of my mind for the moment, I turned to face him as Enzo took up a position beside him in a show of solidarity. "What is it?" I asked, glancing between the two of them.

It was Tristan who spoke. "I want to talk about Veda."

Instantly, my gut clenched. He didn't need to say anymore. I turned and started back toward the house, shouting over my shoulder, "What happened? Is she alright?"

"Luca! Wait! She's fine. Nothing's happened."

I swung back around. "Then what the fuck are you making me stand out here in the heat for?" Holy shit, I was so fucking ready for summer to end.

Tristan stood silently, waiting for me to come back.

"Luca," Enzo said. "You might want to listen to us."

But the thing was, I didn't. Because I could tell by the way they were both looking at me that whatever the fuck they had to tell me was about to change things between me and my *vita*. And, goddamn it, I'd just gotten her back.

I let none of this show on my face, however, as I walked back to them. I crossed my arms over my chest. "I'm listening."

"Don't you think it's strange that your brother just suddenly gave her back to you unharmed?"

"She wasn't unharmed," I corrected.

"Did she say something to you?" Enzo asked.

"No." I shook my head. "But she's not okay. She's not herself."

"She was alive," Tristan said. "That's all that matters."

I looked at him like he'd lost his mind. "Mario is a fucking psychopath. I have no idea what he did to her while she was there, but I can guarantee the time she spent with him wasn't something any of us would like to go through. So no. I wouldn't say that she was unharmed."

"He didn't kill her," Tristan repeated. "Why do you think that is?"

"Because it was more fun for him to give her back to me the way he did. So I would go fucking crazy wondering what happened."

"Did you ever consider that he turned her?"

My eyes snapped to Tristan.

He held up his hand. "Hear me out."

"What the fuck are you saying?" I asked him. "And you'd better think very fucking carefully before you answer that question."

But Tristan wasn't intimidated by my tone or the tension in my shoulders. He never was.

"I'm saying how do we know she isn't a spy for your brother?"

My fist flew through the air and smashed into the side of his face. I hit him so hard his entire body fell back into the SUV. I didn't think before I did it. I just reacted to the eruption of red-hot rage in my blood.

"Hey! Hey!" Enzo jumped between us, but I shoved him out of the way.

Grabbing Tristan by the hair, I yanked his head up to mine. "Don't you ever fucking talk about her like that. Do you hear me?" Then I shoved him back into the side of the car.

Tristan spit a wad of blood onto the ground. "You don't think it's true?"

"No," I ground out. "I don't."

"Then what are you so fucking mad about? Huh?"

Enzo stepped between us. "Luca, just think it through before you go flying off the handle."

"Little late for that," Tristan muttered.

"You." I stuck my finger in his face. "Shut the fuck up."

"Jesus Christ, would you stop?" Enzo yelled.

I spun on my heel and paced a few steps away. I couldn't get enough air in this fucking heat.

"Luca, I don't think Tris is out of line. It's a possibility, and you know it."

"If Veda is a fucking rat, then why the hell hasn't she come out of the bedroom?" I challenged them. "Why doesn't she ever ask me any questions? I don't think she even knows what I do. Not really. No." I shook my head. "No. She's a victim of this fucked up relationship between me and my brother. That's it."

Tristan caught my eye, and my attention was immediately diverted to him. I closed the distance between us. "You ever say shit about her again, and I'll cut out your fucking tongue. *Comprendere?*" I knew I was only focusing on him because he was the one who'd actually had the guts to say what they both were thinking, but I didn't give a fuck. "And you stay the fuck away from her from now on."

He stood toe to toe with me and didn't back down. "You're being unreasonable," he said calmly. "Thinking with your cock instead of your head."

With a roar, I shoved him back into the car and hauled back my fist to hit him again. But Enzo caught my arm and pulled me away from him. "Get off of me!" My eyes never left Tristan. I couldn't have said why I was so hellbent on kicking his ass. All I knew was it made sense in my twisted head.

"Not until you calm the fuck down," Enzo told me. When I continued to struggle, he held both arms behind my back. "Look what you're fucking doing, Luca! You're trying to beat the fuck out of one of the only two people who've stuck by you. And why? Because he's trying to look out for you? This guy, who took a fucking bullet for you. More than once! How does this make any fucking sense?"

It didn't. I knew that. It made no fucking sense at all. But right now, the only thing I wanted to do was get him on the ground and beat his face into a bloody pulp in the dirt.

Tristan walked up to me and got right in my face. And it wasn't because Enzo was holding me back. He'd do this shit even if he wasn't. "You wanna kick my ass, Luca? That's fine. We can take this into the gym if it'll help you get all this pent-up anger out of your system. Because you're not fucking mad at me. It's Mario you want to go after. I know that. And you know that. But I'm here for you, either way."

He was absolutely right. "Let me go," I told Enzo. "Let me go!"

"Go ahead," Tristan told him.

Stepping back, he held up both hands as I yanked my arms out of his hold.

"We're just trying to look out for you, man," Tristan told me.

"She's not a fucking rat."

He nodded. "Okay."

"She wasn't fucking turned."

"Okay."

"She was fucking hurt."

"All right."

"And we're gonna pretend like this conversation never fucking happened." I looked back and forth between the two of them, making sure they understood.

Tristan nodded as I heard Enzo say, "Got it."

"Are we done here?"

Tristan looked over my shoulder at Enzo, and then he nodded. "Yeah, man. We're done."

"Good." Leaving them both standing there, I went into the house and headed right to the gym. I was still fucking starving. But right now, I didn't want to see their fucking faces.

Or anyone's.

CHAPTER 10

LUCA

Nearly a week had passed since I'd gotten Veda back. I rarely saw her during the day, just a glance now and then as she went out to the kitchen, the pool, or grabbed a book from the shelves in the media room. Oftentimes she had a bottle of some kind of strong alcohol in her hands that she must've pilfered from my stash in the kitchen. She didn't seem to have a preference as to what kind it was. The only one she spoke to was Lisa, and I would often catch her watching Veda with a worried expression.

At night, she was usually already in bed when I got there. The few times I'd arrived a little early, she'd barely said two words to me as she brushed her teeth and changed her clothes. Always hidden from me behind closed doors.

She barely spoke to me at all when we were alone, even if I asked her a direct question, so I had Enzo ask her about what had gone down while she was at Mario's, thinking maybe she would open up to him. She told him everything she could remember about the apartment he'd taken her to and what she'd overheard him and his men talking about. When he asked her if he had hurt her, she'd given him the same answer she'd given me the night he'd dumped her at Lisa's.

"Nothing that won't heal."

I didn't push her for anything more, allowing her the time she needed to process everything that had happened. Except when we were in bed. Every night, I would get in beside her and pull her into my arms and hold her. And she would let me do it without argument. I never asked for anything else, but I needed that physical connection with her. And so did she, whether she knew it or not. I felt the way she would relax in my arms. How her breathing would even out. Sometimes she even let out a little moan of relief.

I think some part of me was afraid that if I didn't give her some kind of a tether to hang onto, no matter how fragile, she would lose herself to the events of the last few months. And then *I* would lose *her*.

But by the second week she'd been home, my patience had worn thin. She'd done nothing but mope around this house for weeks, barely speaking and showing no interest in anything or anyone. She wasn't trying to escape anymore. Wouldn't even sit and have a cup of tea with Lisa like she used to. She was a fucking ghost haunting my home, even though she was walking and talking and breathing. And I couldn't stand it. I wanted my *vita* back. She could scream at me if she needed to. Hit me. Run from me. I didn't care. I could handle her emotions. What I couldn't take anymore was watching this empty shell of a woman withdraw into herself until she disappeared.

That night, I finished my work early and was waiting for her when she came upstairs. She'd had enough time to be in her feelings. This shit was stopping now. She was here. She was alive. And maybe I was a selfish ass, but I wanted her back. I didn't stop to analyze this driving force inside of me, or what it would mean for me and my position in the family if kept her as my own. I wasn't weak for wanting a woman. I was fucking human. Every man I knew, including my father, constantly had a woman on his arm. So why the fuck was I the one he pointed his finger at? Was I less of a *uomo muscoloso*, less of a macho man, because I didn't treat her like a whore?

As soon as she walked in, I rose from the end of the bed where I'd been waiting. "I've had enough of this. What the fuck is wrong with you?"

She didn't even look at me on her way to the closet to get her nightclothes.

"Veda. I'm fucking talking to you."

"I don't want to talk to *you*." Her voice was quiet, subdued.

"Goddammit!" I stabbed my fingers into my hair. I was so done being patient with her. This shit was gonna stop. And it was gonna stop right fucking now, if it took us all damn night to hash through this shit.

She jumped at my outburst, her eyes flying to my face. For just an instant, I would swear there was a flash of fear there, but she quickly dropped them again and disappeared inside the closet. When she came out, a clean set of nightclothes in her hands, I was ready for her.

Stepping in front of the bathroom door, I held up my hand. "Stop."

"I want to get changed."

"You can do that when we're done here."

She heaved a heavy sigh, like I was wasting her fucking time, but stayed where she was.

I lowered my hand. "I'm not going to live like this anymore. In my own home. With you skulking about this house like a zombie or some shit." I stopped abruptly. Tried to calm myself. Lowering my voice, I tried to catch her eyes. "Talk to me, Veda."

Instead of doing as I asked, she clenched her jaw and stared at something on the wall behind me.

"What the fuck is going on with you?" I repeated, ducking my head so she had to look at me. But she turned her head, refusing to meet my eyes. "TALK to me." My heart was pounding so loud in my ears I didn't know if I'd even be able to hear her, and for a few seconds I thought she wasn't going to answer me anyway. But then she squared her shoulders and her head snapped up. A storm of emotion darkened her gray eyes. At the sight of her like this, with her eyes flashing and her chest rising and falling with every rapid breath, my own blood ran fast in response, my cock swelling until the zipper of my pants dug into the tender flesh.

There she is.

"What's the matter with me?" she asked incredulously. I could smell the vodka on her breath. "What's the matter with *me?* Do I really need to spell it out for you, Luca? I don't want to *fucking* be here! I don't want to be anywhere near you. I want to go home! I want to live my life without being passed around like a...a..." She threw her hand in the air, floundering. "I'm a PERSON, dammit! I want to get the hell out of this house! Is that clear enough for you?"

Finally, we were getting somewhere. "That's not going to happen. You're not going anywhere."

"Why? Why not? Haven't you done enough?"

She practically spit the words at me, and they hit me hard, right in the fucking gut. But I shoved down the pain they caused. She was just lashing out. "Because you belong here. With me. This is your home now." I didn't deserve her. I knew this. But by all that was holy, this woman was mine. And I wasn't letting her go again.

She laughed out loud. "With you? The man who kidnapped me, dressed me up like another woman to parade around in front of his friends, and then planned to kill me for his petty revenge?" Her smile, beautiful and bitter as it was, fell from her face. "Why the hell would I ever choose to be anywhere near you?"

"Because I'm the only option you have!" The words burst from me in a fit of temper.

She stared up at me for a long time. "No," she said softly. "No, you're not."

Fear twisted my bowels. "Veda…" I said quietly. "Don't ever fucking talk like that. You hear me?"

The life drained from her as quickly as it had appeared. I saw it happen with my own eyes, like a balloon deflating. Dropping her eyes, she shuffled around me and into the bathroom, shutting the door behind her. I heard the lock click.

My fists clenched at my sides and took four steps away from the door, barely stopping myself from spinning around and punching a hole through it. As she got ready for bed, I stared out the window, not seeing the dance of lights across the lake that normally brought me such a sense of peace. Fed up with her, myself, and this entire fucking situation, I turned on my heel and walked out.

But I stopped just outside the bedroom. No. This was bullshit. I'd tried giving her space, and it hadn't done any fucking good. If anything, it only gave her a reason to withdraw even more.

No. I was done giving her her space.

Marching back into the room, I went into the closet and started pulling her clothes off the hangers and out of the drawers, piling them up on the bed. When I had everything, I grabbed an armful and took them down to my room—what would now be OUR room—and threw them into my closet. I wanted to sleep in my own bed. And I wanted Veda there with me.

She was standing beside the bed, staring down at her things, when I came back to get another armful. Ignoring her as she liked to do to me, I gathered up more of her clothes and took them to my room. I heard her footsteps following me.

"What are you doing with my stuff?" she asked from behind me.

I didn't respond. Just turned into our room and threw them on the floor of the closet with the rest. She didn't want to talk to me? Fine. She didn't have to. But I wasn't going to allow her to run away from me anymore. Not even to a spare bedroom down the hall. And I wasn't going to continue sneaking in there at night like a goddamned teenager. This was her home now. And this was her room. With me. Where she belonged. There were no other options. Not now. Not after everything.

"Luca! Why are you bringing my clothes in here? I want to stay in the guest room."

Brushing past her, I went back and got her shoes from the closet, throwing them on the bed. I left everything there that I'd bought for "Nicole." That was the woman I'd needed her to be. Not the woman I wanted.

In the bathroom, I grabbed the trashcan, took out the bag and set it on the floor, then started filling it with her toothbrush, toothpaste, mouthwash, shampoo, and conditioner. Opening a drawer, I found her hairbrush, some hair ties, and her birth control pills and threw them in the trash can. Checking under the sink, I found what was left of a box of tampons Lisa must've picked up for her and threw them in too. Then I walked back into the bedroom, tucked a few pairs of her shoes under my arm, picked up the other pair in my free hand, and took it all back to our room.

Veda watched me in silence as I moved her out of the spare bedroom, but didn't follow me this time. Once her things were all in my room, I went back to collect her. She'd gotten into bed and pulled the comforter up over her head.

Without a word, I yanked it down and lifted her into my arms. Surprisingly, although she was stiff as a board in my arms, she didn't try to struggle. I have to admit, I was disappointed. A fight would've done us both good.

When we got to our room, I kicked the door shut behind me. Then I just stood there in the middle of the floor, my chest heaving with the whirlwind of emotions banging against my ribcage, Veda held tight in my arms. I should've put her down, but I couldn't bring myself to do it. When I felt like I could breathe, I looked down at her.

She was completely still. Waiting for what I would do next. Her arms crossed over her chest and tears rolling silently down her cheeks as she stared at nothing.

The anger I'd been carrying around dissipated on a softly spoken curse. Carefully, I set her on her feet and took her timeless, beautiful, sad face between my hands. "Don't cry, *amore*. Please don't cry." It was on my tongue to tell her I was sorry, but I knew the words would mean nothing. Not now. Not after all the things I'd done. I pressed a soft kiss to her temple, then her cheek, then the corner of her mouth. "Veda." Her name was a plea. A wish. A prayer. "*Vita*...my life. Please come back to me."

I took her bottom lip between my teeth, nipping the soft flesh before pulling it into my mouth to soothe the hurt. I continued to kiss her, soft nipping bites in between soft brushes of my lips until she was forced to respond.

Her hands wrapped around my wrists, and she gave them a tug. But it was a weak effort, and I wouldn't let her go. Finally, with a shuddering breath, she gave in to me, tightening her grip as she parted her lips and let me in. I took full advantage, plunging my tongue into her sweet mouth and kissing her until her lips were red and swollen and she stopped trying to pull away.

Sliding my hands through the soft strands of her hair, I held her mouth to mine, taking what I needed. My blood was on fire, raging through my body, my cock so swollen I seriously wondered if I'd last long enough to get inside of her. I wanted to taste her. Everywhere.

"Touch me," I ordered roughly against her lips. Not giving her the chance to deny me, I took one of her hands and pressed it against my swollen sex. "Do you feel what you *do* to me?" My hand over hers, I forced her to grip me tighter. "You drive me fucking insane, *amore*."

She made a small, helpless noise, but didn't try to pull away.

Flattening her palm, I rolled my hips, rubbing my length against her palm as I continued to kiss her, our very fucking souls mingling with every breath. But it felt so good I had to stop before I came in my pants, taking her hand away with a groan of disappointment that matched hers. Leaving her luscious mouth, I dropped kisses across her jaw to her ear. "I need you, Veda." I let her hear the raw hunger inside of me. With my other hand still in her hair, I forced her head back, exposing her throat. She closed her eyes and laced her fingers through mine, her other hand fisting in my shirt.

I sucked the tender skin of her neck until the blood rose to the surface and stayed. I wanted to mark her everywhere. With my tongue, my teeth, my come. Until there was no doubt in her mind who she belonged to.

She whispered my name, and I was completely fucking lost.

CHAPTER 11

VEDA

I'd forgotten what it was like...

To be possessed by Luca.

How it made me forget where I was and everything he'd done. Everything that had happened to me. Even when I wasn't half lit on vodka, it was like this. The moment he kissed me, everything else disappeared...except for him. The heat of his mouth. The possessive grip of his hands. The way he curled his big body around mine until the only thing in my world was him. His smell. His heat. His taste. I wanted him to crawl under my skin until there was no one and nothing else in the world except for us and the raging fire in our blood.

And this is why there were no warning bells that went off when his large palms slid down over my hips, squeezing my ass as he moaned in my mouth before sliding up under my shirt to spread across the bare skin of my back. It was why I didn't panic when I felt a touch of cool air on my stomach just before he pulled my tee up and off. And it was why I arched my back, offering him my swollen breasts without remembering what he would see. My nipples hard and straining for the feel of his tongue.

It wasn't until my lust-hazed brain realized he'd gone utterly still that it all came crashing back to me.

The pain.

The blood.

The screams.

"What the fuck is this, *amore?*"

His voice was deathly quiet. I don't think I'd ever heard him sound so emotionless. And yet...not. I realized I was shaking, and this time it was terror that held me. His thumb brushed over the skin near the top of my left nipple, just high enough to touch the still healing wound, and I flinched before I could stop myself.

"Veda."

My name was a softly spoken command I couldn't resist, and I slowly raised my tearful eyes to his.

"Who did this to you?"

But I didn't have to answer. It was quite obvious who had carved the letter "M" into my chest. The perfectly straight lines started just above one nipple, went to my collarbone, and ended at the other nipple, with the upside-down peak in the center of my breastbone. He had taken his time. He'd wanted to make sure he didn't fuck it up, since I'd now be wearing it forever.

That's what he'd told me as three of his men held me down. It had happened the same day he'd made that horrific phone call to Luca, threatening to kill me. Mario's eyes had been as crazed as the things coming out of his mouth. His hands had been rough on my naked breasts, the knife sharp enough to cut deep into my skin, but dull enough to feel like a branding iron as he slowly dragged it through my flesh. I'd screamed until I was lightheaded. I'd screamed until I had no voice, and even then, I didn't stop.

And when he was done, when I was lying there with my shirt ripped away, broken and bloody on the floor, wretched noises coming from my sore throat as I'd sobbed, he'd thrown my shirt and bra at my face and left me bleeding on the floor.

It seemed to set something off within him. For three days after, he ranted and raved as he'd paced around the apartment. Every time I happened to cross his path, he'd tear my shirt open so he could stare at the bloody mutilation he'd left on me. Sometimes he'd hunt me down to do it, and he'd always find me. When it scabbed over, he'd tug at my skin with his fingernails until it bled again, staining my clothes. There was nowhere for me to go. Nowhere to hide. Even his own men stayed out of his way.

Finally, on the last day, he told me to get my shoes on, then tied my hands in front of me and threw me into the back of the same van that brought me here.

We drove for a long time, and then they dropped me in a rural area in the middle of the night, pushing me out of the van so hard I'd stumbled and fallen to my hands and knees. Dirt flew into my face as the van spun around and left me alone. I watched them leave, their faces seared into my brain.

The freshly opened wound on my chest screamed with every move I made, and my eyes shifted around nervously in the dark. I used my teeth to loosen the knot and untie the rope around my hands. My breasts and stomach were wet with half dried blood from being tossed around on the floor of the van, and I pressed my shirt to my skin and tried to mop up what I could. Then I started walking the same way the van had gone, barely reacting every time I heard the crack of a branch or the flutter of wings. I was in survival mode, my thoughts carefully blank, other than finding help.

I didn't have to go very far before I came to a small house. Stumbling up to the door, I knocked until I couldn't feel my knuckles anymore. As I did, I constantly looked over my shoulder, thinking this was all just too easy. He was changing the rules of the game, and it terrified me. He was going to change his mind and come back for me.

I nearly fell through the doorway when an average-looking man with broad shoulders and deep-set brown eyes opened the door, his wife right behind him, still pulling on her robe. I nearly fainted with relief when I recognized Lisa. She loaned me a new shirt—long-sleeved and black at my request, to hide any bleeding until I could clean up better—and after I washed off in the little bathroom off the hall, I made her swear she wouldn't tell Luca I was injured. The shirt I'd been wearing I shoved down into the bottom of the half-full trashcan. I couldn't say now why I did that. I just knew I didn't want him to see it.

When I came out, she took me into the kitchen and offered me some tea. I didn't know she had called Luca until he showed up at her door. But she kept her word and didn't say a thing to him.

Looking at him now, I knew it was foolish of me to think I could hide this from him forever. I reached out with a shaking hand, needing to steady myself, but he took a step back, my shirt still bunched in his fist, his cold stare fixated on my mutilated body.

Part of me wanted to turn around and cover myself so he wouldn't see how ugly I was now. But another part of me —a larger, pissed off part of me—wanted him to see. So I clenched my fists at my sides and forced myself to stay exactly where I was, my cheeks heated and angry tears in my eyes. Let him fucking see. Let him see what his brother had done to me. How he'd scarred me forever, and not just on the outside. Let him see what the stakes were for this god forsaken game they played between them.

Luca was eerily quiet, his face expressionless, his eyes never leaving the initial carved into my chest. But I felt his fury, and I saw the burning need that had brightened his blue eyes turn to icy rage.

"What else did he do to you?" His voice was deceptively calm.

My answer was automatic. The same thing I'd been telling myself over and over again. "Nothing that won't—"

"DON'T tell me that." He cut me off before I could finish. "Tell me what he did. Everything."

But I didn't want to. Because he would never look at me the same. The anger drained out of me as fast as it had come on, leaving me lightheaded. I felt weak. Ashamed. And I knew it was stupid, but I couldn't help it. However, I knew there was no avoiding this conversation. Not anymore, thanks to fucking Mario and his hard on for knives. Much like his brother.

Luca closed his eyes, and when he opened them, there was a flicker of the warm, flesh and blood man. There and gone in a heartbeat. "It's okay, Veda. It's okay to tell me. I just need to hear it. I need to hear it, so I know how much to make him suffer when I rip his fucking heart out of his chest with my bare hands." All of this was said casually, almost conversationally.

"You're scaring me," I whispered as I searched his face for any traces of the man I knew. The one who'd held me so tenderly all these nights. But he wasn't there. And neither was the one who'd had me kidnapped and brought to this house. I didn't know this man in front of me.

He didn't try to assuage my fears. He said nothing at all. Just waited. And I knew he would wait all night if he had to.

"Um..." Jesus, how the hell was I supposed to do this? "He...uh..." I swallowed. "Can I have my shirt?"

"No."

I crossed my arms over my naked breasts, half expecting him to scold me. But he allowed me this, at least.

"Start with the first day you were there."

My mind fought against me, not wanting to remember. "Um...he pretty much ignored me the first day."

"Where did you sleep?"

"I didn't," I told him honestly. "But he gave me a room. For the first few nights, he was too busy to worry much about me. All he did was hole up in his office with his thug buddies and try to figure out ways to draw you into his trap."

He stared down at me, and his voice was raw when he said, "I wouldn't have left you there if I could've found you. But I didn't know where he'd taken you. I never stopped looking."

"I know." And I did. If for no other reason than his own goddamned pride, he would've come after me if he could have.

"Did you hear his plans?"

"I told Enzo all of this…"

"Tell me again."

I tried to think. "No. Nothing specific. He was very careful to make sure I only heard just enough," I told him with a bitter smile.

He still hadn't moved or raised his voice. And he still had an erection. "And then?"

I took a deep breath. "And then he told me to go take a shower, and I had to take out the contacts because they were killing my eyes. I'd been there a couple of days…"

"What happened in the shower, Veda?"

He stood there in front of me, his feet slightly apart and arms hanging straight down at his sides. The only thing that gave him away was that his hands were clenched into tight fists. I opened my mouth, but nothing came out. I tried again. "He knew I wasn't her. He knew I wasn't Nicole. He said he'd known since we first got to the apartment because he could tell I was afraid of him, and my sister was too stupid to be afraid of him."

"Is that true?"

"Probably, yes. She thought too much of herself to think any man wouldn't be just as enthralled when he looked at her."

"I meant, is it true that you were afraid."

I looked up at him. "I was fucking terrified, Luca. What the hell else would I be?"

He was quiet for so long this time, I started to shift my weight from foot to foot as an uneasy shiver slid up my spine.

"What did he do then?" he finally asked.

This time, I couldn't look at him. But neither could I lie. He would know if I lied. "I don't want to tell you that," I told him honestly.

"I know you don't. But I need you to."

I sighed with defeat, because I knew damn well he would keep me here wearing nothing but my sleep shorts until he was satisfied I'd told him everything. "He, uh..." I tried to swallow past the swollen ache in my throat. "He tried to force me onto my knees. But I remembered what Enzo taught me and I let myself fall. He fell on top of me and hit his face on the wall."

"And then what?"

"I ran," I whispered. "But I didn't know where I could go. And I wasn't fast enough."

He was quiet for a long time. "And then?"

"And then…" I glanced up at him. A muscle jumped in his jaw. But I couldn't look at him as I said it, so I stared at the center of his chest. "And then he made me suck him off." His breathing was deep and even beneath his black shirt, and somehow it helped that he was so calm. My mouth twisted in disgust as I remembered. "I threatened to bite it off, but he told me he'd put a bullet in my head." I drew in a shaky breath. "I didn't want to do it. I swear I didn't. But I decided being dead was infinitely worse than being forced to give some guy a blow job, so I stopped fighting."

After a few seconds, Luca asked, "Did he hit you?" When I hesitated, he said, "I saw the bruising on your cheek when you first got here."

"Yes. A few times."

"What else did he do?"

I looked away as I felt the blood drain from my face.

"Did he rape you?"

Stunned by the bluntness of his question, I shook my head. "No. He wanted to. He tried. But he couldn't bring himself to do it." Memories filled my head, and it was almost like I was there again, hearing Mario's grunts and curses as he wrestled me onto the bed and tore the clothes from my body. I blinked fast, bringing myself back to the here and now.

"What do you mean?" he asked. "He *couldn't?*" There was a spark of genuine curiosity in his eyes. I'd have been hurt if I didn't also hear the underlying fury in his voice.

I thought about it for a few seconds. "I think he wanted... no...I think he *needed* me to be her. And I'm just...not."

He appeared to steel himself in preparation for my answer before he asked the next question. "What about his men? Did they"—there was the slightest hesitation—"touch you?"

I shook my head. "Not really. He wouldn't let them. I think he has some kind of twisted sense of loyalty because Nicole was my sister." I didn't tell him they were only allowed to touch me when he needed them to hold me down. "I heard you on the phone," I told him quietly as I finally found the courage to look straight at him. "I heard what you said."

He gave me a pained stare. "You understand I couldn't let him know what you mean to me? If I had...Veda, he would've killed you. I couldn't take that chance. I was trying to buy myself some time."

I nodded. "I know." Luca was right. Mario would've carried out his threat to put a bullet between my eyes. But I still couldn't help but wonder...

"Is there more?"

I shook my head. Oh, there were other things I could tell him. I could tell him how after the scene in the shower, I would wake up in the morning to Mario masturbating next to my bed and coming on my face, his other hand under the silky gown I slept in and his fingers shoved painfully inside of me. I could tell him how sometimes he would stare at me for a long time as we sat at the table, until the sight of me—looking so much like Nicole and yet not being her—made him so angry he would drag me out of my chair and throw me across the room. I could tell him how I was his brother's emotional punching bag for the guilt that ate him alive inside. How I knew that, in his own sick way, Mario had really loved my sister and felt like he'd had no choice but to kill her once she exposed their engagement on national television, and therefore, his location. And how, even knowing that, I felt no pity for him.

But telling Luca all of that wouldn't change what had happened. It wouldn't change Mario's future. He knew enough.

"Thank you for telling me," he told me.

"What are you going to do?"

His fists unclenched, my shirt falling to the floor as he flexed the stiffness from his long fingers, then raised them to the top button of his shirt. Slowly, his eyes never leaving mine, he slid the button through the hole, then moved on to the next one. "Right now, I'm going to fuck you, Veda. Because I have to. Because you're mine. Because I can't stand having you so close to me and not being inside of you any longer." He paused. "Because you need this, too."

I stared up at him. His jaw was tense. His eyes like an arctic glacier. "What if I don't want you?"

He cocked his head, one side of his mouth lifting into a cocky smile, his blue eyes dark with something I'd never seen there before. Possession. Yeah, there was that. Even more so now that I told him everything that had happened. But it was more than that. Hatred. The desire to hurt something...

It scared me.

Would he let me go if I insisted? I almost laughed out loud at the naive girl inside of me who thought there was any chance of that.

As I watched him reveal himself to me, the fire that had burned down to embers with his endless questions flared to life again. He was right. I needed this. I needed him to help me forget. To replace my memories with Mario with new ones. Yet part of me was disgusted with myself for letting him get back under my skin so easily. The other part wished he would hurry it the hell up before I talked sense into myself, took my shirt back, and walked out of this room.

But underneath it all was the shame I felt. "How can you stand to look at me?" I whispered.

Cold blue eyes dropped down to my chest and then fell lower. He didn't bother to dignify that with an answer. "Take those off." He nodded at my sleep shorts as he shrugged out of his shirt and started unfastening his pants.

"Luca..."

"Take them OFF or I'll fucking rip them from your body."

Trembling with equal parts fear and desire, rage heated my blood. I was tired of being ordered around. Tired of being a pawn in his game. Tired of feeling helpless. I drew myself up to my full height and lifted my chin.

Luca stared at me with the eyes of a predator about to devour its prey.

"No."

CHAPTER 12
LUCA

"No," she said again. Louder this time.

My fingers paused on the fastening of my pants. She was fucking serious as hell, lifted slightly onto the balls of her feet like she was about to sprint out of this room.

Oh, please run, I begged her silently. Adrenaline rushed through my system, making my heart pound and my focus on Veda razor sharp. My cock swelled to bursting. "Take them OFF. Now." I needed to be inside of her ten fucking minutes ago. It had taken everything in me not to flip the goddamn bed into the wall as she told me what Mario had done to her. He may not have straight up raped her, but that didn't mean what she'd gone through didn't haunt her, just as it would now haunt me.

But right now, the only thing I needed was to feel her sweet cunt squeezing my cock. It was almost bestial, this overwhelming urgency to claim her. Possess her. Mark her as mine. To remove every fucking trace of another man's touch from her skin. I wanted her to wear my scent, to only know my touch, my voice, my body. I wanted to mark her like an animal.

Her grey eyes skittered around the room before landing on her shirt I'd dropped onto the floor. With one arm still concealing her perfect tits, she lunged for it. I didn't even try to stop her as she pulled it back over her head. The bemused expression on her face when she realized I was going to give her this temporary piece of power was almost amusing.

Tomorrow, I would burn all of her nightclothes. If I didn't have a house full of people, I'd burn her entire closet and force her to walk around naked. But if anyone here laid their eyes on her luscious curves other than me, I'd have to rip their eyes from their head. Lifelong friend or not.

I watched her, waiting to see what she would do next. She wasn't leaving this room. Fuck no. But her antics were enough to distract me from the desire to cause pain and watch blood run across my bedroom floor. My anger wasn't directed at her. Yet the urge was there. And if I didn't want to hurt her, which I didn't, I needed to blow off steam another way.

Veda was mine. And it was time she remembered that. Time she remembered who she was. The woman who shook my world wasn't this timid little creature in front of me. She was someone who didn't know when to keep her mouth shut. Someone who may be afraid, but who fought back anyway. She was the perfect match for me, and I wanted her back.

"Where are you gonna go, Veda? Huh?"

"Luca, please. I just don't want to do this right now."

Dropping her eyes to the floor, she tried to hide from me.

Fine. She wanted to play it like this? Reaching into my back pocket, I pulled out the small switchblade I kept there at all times. Just in case. The same one I'd threatened her with the first night she arrived.

She jumped when the blade shot out with a click, her eyes flying to the knife in my hand. "What are you doing?"

With one step, I closed the distance between us. Grabbing the neckline of her shirt, I sliced through the material until there was a good-sized cut. Then I grabbed it with both hands and tore it down the middle, ignoring her cry of alarm, exposing her luscious breasts and the half-healed "M" my brother had left there. A red haze dropped over my vision at the sight of it.

Attempting to hold the edges of her shirt together, she retreated until the backs of her legs were up against the mattress. "What the hell are you doing?"

I followed her, standing so close she either had to hold her ground or get on the bed.

She stayed where she was, looking up at me with wide, gray eyes. I saw a spark of anger. Just an ember. But it was enough. I just needed to blow on it a little to bring out the flames.

Laying the flat edge of the knife just beneath her collarbone with the tip of the blade touching a peak of the letter, I asked her, "Should I fix this for you, Veda? It won't take much. With a few small adjustments, I can make it so my *fratello's* mark is unrecognizable." I pressed the tip of the blade into her skin just hard enough that a drop of blood appeared, then slid it down the center of her breastbone between the ragged edges of her shirt, smearing her blood across her smooth skin. "I can make it into a heart. It wouldn't be very pretty. But it would remind you that you are MINE."

"No," she whispered. "Luca, please."

"Why not?"

"Because it'll hurt!" She tried to lean back, but I caught her with an arm around her back.

"Don't you want my mark on you?"

"What?"

She looked up at me like I'd lost my ever-loving mind. And hell, maybe I had, because the sight of that drop of blood excited me. I wanted to see more. I wanted her to have something of *me* carved forever into her skin. Not my fucking brother. I dragged the tip of the knife over the inside curve of her breast, just hard enough to slightly indent her pliant skin. So young. So fresh.

"Luca! Stop!" Her hands gripped the edges of her shirt so hard her knuckles were white, unsure how to stop me without risking a slip of the knife.

"Why?" I asked her. "Does it make you feel weak? Like you have no control?"

She opened her mouth. Closed it again. Tears filled her eyes. But behind them, I saw that spark again. "Why are you doing this?"

"Does it make you angry, Veda? What he did to you? What *I'm* doing to you?"

"Yes," she gritted out between her teeth.

I leaned down until my face was level with hers. "Then fucking show me," I sneered.

For a moment, she was caught with indecision. But then she straightened, her jaw clenched tight, and her mouth twisted with anger.

I smiled when I saw her. My butterfly emerging from her cocoon.

With a growl, she knocked my hand away from her, and I let her do it. Then she shoved both palms against my chest, an angry sob bursting from her.

"Is that all you've got?" I asked her. Grabbing one of her arms, I twisted it up behind her and dragged her in closer until her naked chest was pressed against mine and the blade of my knife was beneath her jaw. Her free hand grabbed my arm and pulled, but I was immovable. "What are you gonna do, Veda? Hmm?" Leaning down, I ran my tongue over the seam of her mouth.

I pulled back just in time to avoid the snap of her teeth. Immediately after, I felt her leg move, and twisted my hips just in time to block her from giving me a full-on knee to the balls, pulling her tighter against me. A delighted laugh burst from me, as dark as my soul. "That's it, my *vita*. Fight. Fight me. You won't win."

"The hell I won't," she swore. She started to struggle, but I had her trapped between me and the bed.

Another drop of blood welled along her jawline where I'd nicked her when she tried to knee me. I licked it clean, pressing a kiss to the small wound before I moved to her sweet mouth and sucked at her bottom lip. She turned her head away, and I kissed her jaw. Her throat. Her shoulder.

She held herself stiff, denying the inferno that burned between us. Without warning, I shoved her back onto the bed and crawled on top of her before she could react, my weight holding her down and my knife still in my hand.

When she tried to get away, I pressed the blade against her throat. "Don't."

She glared up at me, her bare chest rising and falling with each heavy breath. "I hate you," she blurted.

"Good," I told her. "At least you're feeling something."

My finger traced the lines carved into her previously flawless flesh, followed by my mouth. She didn't say a word. Didn't flinch. Even though I knew it had to still hurt. "I'll fucking flay him alive for doing this to you," I murmured with my lips against her mutilated skin.

The tang of her blood still on my tongue and my knife still pressed against her throat, I sucked one hardened nipple into my mouth, taking it between my teeth. I bit her just hard enough to get a reaction, then eased the pain with my lips and tongue before kissing my way over to the other one.

Veda tensed when I reached it, waiting for the pain, and moaning when it never came. In disappointment? Because as much as she tried to play it off like she didn't like this, I saw the way her blood raced, flushing her face and chest. Heard the way her breath caught in her lungs. Running my hand down her ribcage and over the curve of her belly, I slid it beneath the waistband of her shorts to cup her pussy in my palm. I felt the way she relaxed her thighs, parting them just enough to give me room to maneuver while still giving off the facade that she was resisting. I dipped my middle finger between her folds. She was soaking wet. Her clit swollen. I added another finger and pushed them both deep inside of her, moaning as her body tightened around them.

Rising up, I stabbed the knife into the mattress beside her, then yanked her shorts down over her hips and legs. She tried to roll away, but I caught her by the hips and flipped her onto her stomach, then slapped her ass hard enough to leave my palm print.

"Goddammit! Let me go!"

"No," I told her. One hand on the center of her back to hold her in place, I pushed my pants down just far enough to get my cock free, then gripped both her legs and spread them wide. Lowering my weight over her so she couldn't get away, I slid one arm under hips as she cursed me to hell and back and entered her from behind with one stroke, shuddering when her wet heat gripped my swollen cock, her sweet pussy so fucking tight.

Holy fuck. I had to hold off for a few seconds, so I didn't come right then and there.

Veda was like a wild thing beneath me, bucking her hips and clawing at the comforter, screaming at me to get off of her. But I couldn't, even if I fucking wanted to. Which I didn't.

Holding myself up on one forearm, I pulled out and then pushed back in, deeper this time, until I was balls deep. With a growl, I started to fuck her in earnest, the feel of her sweet pussy squeezing my cock too much, and unable to help myself, I sank my teeth into the muscle between her neck and shoulder. Not enough to break the skin. Just enough to hold her beneath me. Sounds I didn't recognize as my own were torn from my throat with every thrust.

Faster and harder, I drove into her. And it still wasn't enough. I pulled out, flipped her over, and entered her again. Veda pushed at my shoulders and screamed in my face, her eyes wild. And I knew it wasn't me she was seeing. Wasn't me she was hitting.

I let her take out her anger on me, just as I was taking out mine on her. "You're mine," I growled into her face. "MINE."

"Fuck you!" she cried, even as her back arched and her body shuddered beneath me.

"Yes," I told her. "Yes, *vita*. Come for me, *amore*. Fucking come for me. NOW, Veda. Fuck...now!"

With a cry, she obeyed me, her body jerking and her pussy contracting around my cock. I came so hard nothing coherent came out of my mouth. I was like an animal, thrusting deep, emptying myself deep inside of her as my arms gave out and I collapsed on top of her.

For a few seconds, I couldn't move, dragging ragged breaths in and out of my lungs. Then I rolled off of her and pulled her against me until she was sprawled across my chest, both of us panting as we tried to catch our breath.

"I hate you," she whispered.

"I know, *amore*." Grabbing the edge of the comforter, I pulled it over both of us and held her tight as she fell asleep. Once she was breathing deep and steady, her body relaxed, I reached over and found the knife, closed it, and laid it on the nightstand beside me. Then I turned off the light.

It was a long time before I fell asleep.

CHAPTER 13
VEDA

When I woke up, the sun was shining through the window and Luca was no longer in bed. I rolled over with a yawn, feeling the sting of air hitting the small cut on my jaw that hadn't had time yet to heal, and slowly blinked my eyes open as memories of last night came rushing back. My cheeks burned as I remembered how I'd lashed out at Luca. The crazy thing I'd become in his arms as he'd pushed through the wall I'd built up around myself.

Something was very different now, though. And it wasn't just that I was physically satiated. There was shame for how I'd acted. Embarrassment for how I'd let him play me and how much I'd enjoyed it. But also...a strange sort of peace. All of the pent-up fear and rage that I'd hoarded inside the past few weeks was gone. Exorcised like a demon by Luca's unholy act of lust. I turned my head toward his side of the bed, extending my arm until I could touch his pillow. Too many emotions to name tangled inside of me as I plucked at the edge of the case covering it. I could still smell him in the bed, a mixture of clean soap and some kind of dark spice from whatever he wore on his skin. It made me rub my thighs together in an effort to ease the ache between them, the soreness from last night forgotten with my sudden need to feel his thick cock sinking into me again.

My eyes landed on a tear in the sheets. No, not a tear. The place where he'd stabbed the knife through the sheet and into the mattress. I felt strange as I stared at it. As I remembered the way he'd talked to me and the way I'd responded to his assault on my body. I'd known what he was doing even as it happened, but I couldn't stop my reaction. He'd done it on purpose to draw me out of my comatose state and get a reaction out of me. Made it safe for me to release the pain I'd crushed down inside through blood and sex. And it'd worked. And I...god...

I covered my face with my hands. I'd loved it as much as I'd hated it.

Oh man, I was really fucked up, wasn't I?

Setting all of that aside to think about more later, when I had the bandwidth to process everything, I got up out of bed and stretched, feeling the inconsequential aches and pains from last night. In the closet, I picked out a pair of peach, stone-washed, jean shorts and a navy tee with an image of Janis Joplin on the front and seriously debated hauling everything else back to the guest room I'd been staying in. But in the end, I didn't have the energy for this particular battle right now, and I hung up the rest where there was space. Luckily, I didn't need much. Then I shoved my underwear into one of the empty built-in drawers, keeping a comfy cotton set of pink hi-cut briefs with a plain matching bra to wear that was cut in a way it shouldn't irritate my chest.

As I walked in front of the bathroom mirror, I caught a glimpse of myself. I stilled, and slowly turned to face it. There were a few new bruises from Luca's rough hands last night where he'd gripped my arms, and a good-sized one on my thigh. Wasn't sure how that one got there. There was also a small nick on my jaw from the blade of his knife, but surprisingly, nothing else. It looked like no more than a scratch, or maybe a paper cut, in the light of morning.

As much as I told myself not to look, my eyes fell of their own accord to the "M" carved into my chest. I didn't look at it any more than I absolutely had to now. The day it happened though, I'd stood in the bathroom for two hours, staring at this new part of me, too shocked to cry and too scared to scream. It was healing pretty well since I'd gotten back to Luca's, but there were still quite a few areas that were scabbed over. I wondered how bad it would scar. Right now, it was raised and red and ugly, but I hoped that would calm down with time. Maybe even fade to a point it would be barely noticeable.

Before I could start freaking out again, I quickly brushed my teeth and got into the shower. The hot water stung my chest, but I forced myself to stay under the spray, wincing as I added soap and started washing myself. I don't know what I was hoping for. That maybe if I scrubbed hard enough, I could remove enough layers of skin to make it disappear? Or at least wash away the nightmares? Either way, it didn't work. Carefully thinking about nothing at all, I finished my shower and shut off the water.

When I stepped out, Luca was there, holding my towel out for me. I hadn't even heard him come in. I eyed the long scratches on the left side of his neck and his swollen right eye where the skin was beginning to discolor, then took it from him without a word. I didn't bother to try to hide my nakedness from him. He'd already seen all there was to see of me. Inside and out. There was no reason to hide anymore.

He was dressed casually today in dark jeans and a maroon T-shirt, his face clean shaven and his loafers on his feet. His eyes fell to the bruises on my arms and leg, then locked onto my chest for a few seconds before he looked away, but other than a muscle ticking in his jaw, he gave no reaction. "How are you feeling?" he asked me.

"I'm fine."

He watched me silently as I toweled myself off. "I brought you something." Then he walked over to the bathroom counter and picked up a jar.

Curious, I wrapped the towel around me and tucked the end inside just above my breasts as I followed him. He was holding a jar of petroleum jelly.

"This will help your cuts heal with minimal scarring." Taking off the top, he dipped two fingers inside and started spreading the stuff on the cuts on my chest. His expression was carefully neutral, but I didn't miss the tightness of his jaw or the flare of anger in his blue eyes as he spread it carefully over my skin. "I called my physician first thing to ask him if there was anything we could do. Plastic surgery, maybe, at some point. But as it's already started to heal, the most we can do right now is try to minimize the scar tissue. And hopefully it will just fade over time."

"I can always get a tattoo."

One eyebrow went up in disapproval. "I would never let you desecrate your body that way."

So that would explain why he was one of the few men I knew who didn't have any art on his skin. "It's not your choice," I informed him.

"Isn't it, Veda?"

I didn't bother to fight with him. Although I felt better after a good night's sleep and a shower, I was still mentally exhausted. Instead, I stood in front of him and let him put the ointment on me, loosening my towel when he ordered me to so he could get the entire thing. When he was finished, he dabbed a little on the nick on my jaw.

Out of nowhere, tears welled in my eyes, and I tried to blink them back before he could see. But, of course, he noticed. Luca noticed everything.

"What's this?" he asked as one escaped. Cupping the side of my face in one hand, he brushed it away with his thumb.

I just shook my head. "Nothing. I'm just feeling sorry for myself."

"It'll fade, *amore*."

I tried for a smile, and failed miserably. "I know."

"We're supposed to cover this with bandages—"

He started to walk away to find some, but I stopped him with a hand on his arm. "That's okay. The tape irritates my skin. I can just put more on when I need to."

"Are you sure?"

"Yeah." I paused, still hanging onto his arm with one hand while the other kept my towel from falling, and met his eyes. "Thank you," I told him sincerely. I wasn't just talking about the petroleum jelly, and I could see by the way he fell completely still that he knew it.

He stared at me for a long moment, his eyes dipping to my chest until he tore them away. In a steely voice, he said, "Get dressed and come down to my office. We have some things to discuss."

My hand slid down his arm as he left, and even though his expression was still cold, he gave my hand a quick squeeze before leaving me alone, so brief, I wondered if I'd only imagined it. The bedroom door shut quietly behind him. For a long time after he left, I just stood there in the middle of the bathroom, wondering what the hell was happening between us. We'd marked each other deeply last night, and not just physically. And I knew I wasn't the only one who felt it.

Straightening my spine and taking a deep breath, I combed out my wet hair and stuck it up on top of my head in a messy bun. Or at least it would be when it dried. Then I finished in the bathroom and got dressed. As I passed by the closet door, I stopped and looked inside at the things I'd hung up earlier. Nothing from "Nicole" was there. Just the things I liked to wear, few as they were. It was all summer stuff, and I wondered if now that the gig was up, if he'd let me get the rest of my things from my apartment. Or better yet, let me go home. Eventually. I held onto hope that I could talk him into it. I needed some space. To be my myself, away from his overpowering presence. If I still had a home to go home to and hadn't been evicted by now.

There was only one way to find out. Pulling the blankets up on the bed, I went to go get some coffee and find Luca.

As I traipsed through the house, I had a feeling of familiarity. Of comfort. But I shook it off. This beautiful house was not my home. It was a cage, albeit one where the caretakers were all pretty nice for the most part. But still a cage.

The door to his office was closed when I got there a few minutes later. Switching my coffee to my right hand, I knocked.

"Come in."

I cracked the door and stuck my head inside. "You wanted to talk to me about something?"

Luca held up his finger to tell me to give him a moment and then waved me inside. I stepped into the office and closed the door.

Cell phone to his ear, his eyes took in my hair piled on top of my head, then took a slow, leisurely walk down my body, hesitating on my bare feet before climbing back up to my face. I couldn't read his expression when he got there, but if he didn't like the way I dressed...well, that was too fucking bad.

"Tell my father I'll see him tomorrow. And thanks for taking care of this for me, Frank."

My skin crawled at the name. "Frank" was the name of one of Mario's henchmen. But surely it couldn't be the same man? It was a popular name, after all.

Taking the cell away from his ear, he tapped the screen and set it face down on his desk. "Come sit down, Veda."

I chose one of the leather chairs in front of his desk. It was chilly in his office, or maybe it was just the vibe in the air that made me shiver. The hot-blooded man of the night before was nowhere to be found this morning, along with the man who had so gently tended to me not an hour before, and in his place was someone with ice running through his veins. The man who'd had his thugs steal me from my sister's apartment and bring me here.

The man who'd wrapped his hands around my throat and cut off the air from my lungs when I dared to strike him. I stared at him across the wide expanse of his desk, feeling oddly comforted by the personality switch. This man, I knew. This man, I could deal with.

I set my cup down on his desk, crossed my legs and arms and returned his stare, waiting for him to speak.

He seemed to have something on his mind, but then he shifted in his chair, turning it sideways, and crossed one ankle over his knee. Turning his head to stare out the window, he asked, "Now that you're home and have come back to the land of the living, I feel it's necessary to remind you of the rules for your situation."

"I'm sorry?" I asked, pretty sure I hadn't heard him correctly.

He turned his chair around so he faced me, leaning into the high back. He looked exactly like the mafia lord he was. Like something out of a movie. Oozing danger and sex appeal that my body immediately responded to. "Is this something we need to go over again?" he asked.

It took me a second to get over the shock. "I don't want to live here. I want to go home to my apartment."

He sighed heavily, rubbing his forehead with the tips of his fingers like just my presence in his office was already giving him a headache. "I told you last night, that's not possible."

"Why not? You don't need me anymore, and the only thing I want is to get as far away from all of this"—I threw my arms around, encompassing him, his office, the entire house, and all of the shit that'd come with it—"as humanly possible."

"Because you know too much now, Veda," he told me. And I could tell by his tone that he was barely holding on to his patience. "That hasn't changed. Your life will be in constant danger. My enemies will hunt you like an animal and use whatever means they have to get information out of you."

I didn't know what the hell I'd done between last night and this morning, but something had shifted with him. With us. "I wouldn't tell them anything."

"Yes," he said. "You would." I started to shake my head, and he leaned forward in his chair, placing his elbows on the desk and spearing me with blue eyes suddenly dark with something I couldn't identify. "Have you ever had your teeth pulled out of your skull with nothing to stop you from feeling them being ripped from your gums? Had your fingernails removed slowly one by one by a pair of rusty pliers? Have you ever had your bones broken? Because that's what they would do to you. And if that didn't work, they'd start peeling your skin away until you were nothing but a mass of bloody muscle-covered bones. They'd hold your head beneath water, until you stopped struggling and were sure you were about to drown. They would rape you, Veda. And they wouldn't give a fuck if you were only half alive when they did it."

He stopped. His chest rising and falling and that muscle in his jaw ticking as he visibly tried to get himself back under control. "These are the types of men I deal with on a daily basis, and those are my friends. My enemies are even worse." He sat back in his chair again. "I know you think you've been through some shit since you've met me. But you haven't. Do you still think you wouldn't confess everything you know? Beg them to kill you? If for no other reason than to stop the pain?"

My stomach rolled and clenched, and I fought to keep down the bile rising up my throat, grateful I hadn't eaten anything yet. I didn't answer his question, because he was right. I didn't know if I was strong enough not to spill my guts before they did. "I'll leave town. Get a new name. Color my hair..."

"No!" He seemed as startled as I was by his outburst. "No," he said, calmer now. "You're not coloring your hair again. And you're not running away. You're staying here with me."

"Why?" I demanded loudly as I uncrossed my legs and threw my hands up in the air. "Why not? The game is over, Luca. You have no reason to keep my here anymore. Dammit, I don't *want* to be here!"

He was out of his chair and around his desk before I had a chance to react. Bracing a hand on each arm of my chair, he leaned down until we were face to face. "You will stay here because the only way I can guarantee your safety is if you're with me. And I'm not sending you out there"—he looked out the door of his office with a jerk of his chin—"to be tortured and killed. Here, with me, is the only place you are safe."

But he was wrong. So very wrong. Being with him might keep me alive, but it was by no means safe. Not for either of us.

CHAPTER 14
LUCA

"This is your life now, Veda. With me. And it's time you accepted it."

Fucking stubborn as always, she shook her head. "No. No, it's not. And I don't."

I searched her face. There was a storm brewing in her gray eyes. I was relieved to see it even as I wanted to pull her over my lap and spank her ass until her skin was bright pink. "It's the only choice you have."

"No," she insisted, sticking her face in mine, her sweet mouth so close I could take that full bottom lip between my teeth. "It's not."

Pushing off her chair, I backed away, not believing what I was hearing. "So you'd choose death over living here with me?" Something cracked inside of me. Did she truly hate me that much?

And could I blame her?

"That's not what I meant."

"But that's your only other choice, Veda."

She held my eyes with hers, searching. Always searching. What was she looking for, I wondered? A decent man? A man who would bow down to her demands even when they made no fucking sense? A man who would give up his own selfish needs for her?

She wasn't going to find that man here.

We stood at a standoff until she looked away, picking up her coffee and taking a sip. She drank it sweet and creamy. I knew this about her. Just like I knew she only had one cup of coffee in the morning and then she had water or hot tea the rest of the day. When she was at home, she walked around looking like an adorable *senzatetto*...a homeless person. And honestly, she didn't dress much better when she was in public, but she did brush her hair and put on shoes. And she was a thousand times hotter to me than the women I knew who wouldn't leave their room without giving the illusion of walking right off the cover of a magazine. Veda was real. Inside and out. Those other women were not.

I knew she was competitive when she trained. Enzo had told me how she would keep getting up from the mat, no matter how many times he threw her down, until she managed to do the move that he was showing her correctly. I knew she was smart, and that she'd been wasting that intelligence being her sister's personal slave. The same sister she called for in her sleep, the bond of twins unbroken even in death. She'd only settle down when I pulled her into my arms and soothed her, sighing sweetly against my chest, trusting me to keep her safe even when she wasn't conscious enough to realize she shouldn't.

I wondered if she'd ever call out for me.

"So tell me, Veda, what I'm to do with you, then. Should I lock you in your room? Hmm? Have Lisa bring you meals and wash your clothes? Bar the patio doors so you can't even go out onto the balcony for fear you'll try to leave?"

"No," she whispered with a small shake of her head.

"Then what?" I asked her. "Because there's no way in hell I'm letting you out of this house. I don't need your fucking death on my conscience. Not yours."

She stared at me for a long time. "Could I go live in the smaller house on your property?"

"No."

"Why not?"

"It's occupied," I snapped back at her. Which was true. By Tristan. And there was no fucking way in hell I was letting her stay with another man.

"Can I have my room back?"

I thought about her request. For a brief second. "No."

She huffed out a breath. "I don't understand why I can't have any privacy. If this is to be my...temporary home..."

she stuttered over the words, "then I'd like a space I can call my own."

She was right. I was being obstinate about something that didn't matter in the least. Not really. Why not give her back her own room if that would give her the illusion of having a choice? It wouldn't keep me out.

But the thought of not having her things in my closet, the scent of her shampoo lingering in my shower...it made my guts twist. I'd just gotten her back; I couldn't bring myself to let her go.

I turned away, unable to look at her anymore, and forced myself to look past my own fucked up needs and think about hers. Maybe she was right. Maybe I should let her go. There were ways I could keep her safe and still allow her to have some semblance of freedom. A life without me in it, if that's what she truly wanted. I had the manpower and the connections to get her somewhere safe and keep her that way. This...*obsession* I had with this woman was too distracting, and if I were honest with myself, she was probably in more danger here than she would be off on her own. She was young, and still naive in a lot of ways. This life I led, the one I was dragging her into, it would eat her alive if she stayed here.

Yet, as fast as the idea came, I threw it away, my upper lip lifting in a snarl. The thought of letting her go was like reaching into my guts with my bare hands and ripping out a piece of myself. I just couldn't do it.

I turned back to her. "You have this entire house to call your own. Do whatever you want to it. I don't give a fuck. I'll hire whoever you need, and money is no object. Except for my office and my gym."

She frowned up at me. "You want me to redecorate your house so...what? So it'll keep me occupied?"

"I want you to do whatever it is that will make you happy living *here*. With me."

Shooting me a look that would cause a lesser man to wither where he stood, she rose from her chair and walked over to the table where I kept my best whiskey. Uncapping the bottle, she grabbed a glass.

But I was right behind her. "Other than become a raging alcoholic." Taking the glass from her, I set it back on the tray and re-capped the bottle. "I think you should lay off of this for a while."

"Seriously? What are you now, my dad?"

Something sparked inside of me, and I lost what little patience I'd managed to retain up until this point. Grabbing her wrists, I twisted her arms behind her and yanked her up against me, bending her backward and looming over her like the overbearing asshole I was. "Does your dad kiss you like I do?" I asked her. "Has he tasted every inch of your body? Does he make your pussy so wet you drench his fingers when he touches you?" She turned her face away, and I scraped my teeth along her jawline before growling in her ear, "Does he *fuck* you like I do?"

"No," she whispered.

"No," I repeated. Transferring her wrists to one hand, I ran the other over the curve of her ass, dipping my fingers between her thighs. The fine thread of careful control I'd held on to all morning had snapped.

I hated this forced distance she kept between us. The way she denied what we had. And if I had to stoke the fire within her by force, I would. As many times as I needed to until she accepted that this was right where she belonged.

I nipped at her jaw again, dragging my tongue along the nick from my knife so I could taste the tang of her blood, and felt the scratches she'd left on my throat burn in response.

She turned her head toward mine to break the contact. "I don't want this," she said in a fragile voice.

But my *vita* was not weak. She was strong. She was passionate. She did want this. She wanted me. And she needed to remember that.

Something dark and acrid coated my tongue as another ugly thought forced its way through the chaos in my mind. Was she remembering my brother's hands on her? Was there more that had happened between them while she was there? Things she wasn't telling me? Had he carved out a piece of her to keep when he'd scarred her beautiful flesh? Something primitive and animalistic rumbled deep in my chest and rose to the back of my throat.

What he'd done to her made my stomach heave. And yet she'd showed no fear when I pulled my own knife on her. Twice now I'd drawn blood, and she'd barely flinched.

Had she encouraged him to do this to her? Did it get her off? Had she enjoyed sucking his cock? He hadn't raped her, she'd said. Was that her way of telling me he hadn't needed to?

As these thoughts and more tripped over themselves in my head, everything went red. The small part of me that remained sane knew I was reaching, that these things made no sense. But the other part of me, that primeval part of myself, was louder by far. So loud I wanted to scream with the need to mark Veda as my own as Mario had done.

Dragging her over to the chair she'd just vacated, I sat down, shoving her to her knees in front of me. My cock was already swollen to bursting, aching with the need to come down her throat. To coat her inside and out as mine. "Stay right where you fucking are," I ordered as I undid my pants.

She watched me with wide eyes, but did as I said. When my cock sprang free, so hard the head was thick and purple, her lips parted on a gasp, even as she looked away.

Leaning forward, I grabbed her by the hair she'd piled on top of her head, only vaguely noticing it was still damp from her shower. "Put me in your mouth."

"No." Her jaw was clenched tight.

Pulling her face closer, I rubbed the tip of my cock against her lips, coating them with the drops of come that were already leaking from the tip. "Suck me, Veda." I knew I was acting like a monster. No better than my goddamned brother. But I needed this. I needed her to show me, even if she wouldn't admit it out loud, that it was *me* she craved.

She pressed her lips together.

Furious that she wouldn't accept me, I grabbed the bottom of her shirt and pulled it up and off, tossing it on my desk. The bra she wore was plain and pink. Innocent. It made me pause, but only for a second. I shoved the straps down over her shoulders and arms until the cups folded down and exposed her perfect breasts. She said nothing, didn't fight me or try to get up. She just kneeled there with a mulish expression on her face that only infuriated me more.

The "M" on her chest was still swollen and discolored, with a thin red line down the middle and shiny from the Vaseline I'd applied. My own chest burned as I stared at it, the roar in my ears so loud I could only feel my own pounding heart. Taking my cock in my hand, I ran my palm up and down its length. Then again. A moan escaped me the third time, and I picked up the pace, squeezing my sex in an almost painful grip. I realized Veda was watching me, her lips parted and her breath coming in pants. Yet she held perfectly still, her shoulders tense.

I fell back in the chair as my balls tightened, my eyes on her mouth and tits and my hips lifting with each stroke of my hand. The pressure began at the base of my spine, and I levered my body up to grab her by the hair again. I held her still as my cock pulsed in my hand, my orgasm hitting so fast and hard I yelled out with the intensity of it.

I coated that fucking letter on her chest with my come until it was dripping from her breasts. And when there wasn't a drop left in me, I released my sex and rubbed it into her raw skin, marking her as mine. And only mine.

But it wasn't enough. Wasn't nearly enough. I yanked on her hair until her chin came up and took her lips with mine, forcing her to accept me. When she finally... finally!...opened to me on a moan, I felt my sex begin to harden again. But I pulled my mouth away and rested my forehead against hers. "You make me fucking crazy, *amore*."

She said nothing at all. Didn't move. Didn't try to look at me. And now that I could see something other than the red haze of my anger and jealousy, that bothered me more than her rejection.

I closed my eyes and cursed softly. "I'm sorry," I told her. Taking her face between my palms, I met her eyes. "I'm sorry," I repeated.

"No," she finally said. "You're not. So do me the decency of not lying to me about it."

She was right. I wasn't fucking sorry. Not at all. I fixed her bra straps and handed her her shirt, a surge of satisfaction rushing through me to see my come drying on her mutilated skin.

As soon as she was decent, I pulled her up into my lap and wrapped my arms around her. I sighed, my anger diminished for the moment. "You can't leave me, Veda. I won't allow it."

If she heard the raw need in my voice, she didn't react to it.

She cleared her throat. "Are you happy now?" she asked me. "Does...does...*humiliating* me like this make you feel more like a man? Do you feel better now that you practically pissed all over me like a dog?"

I pulled back and stared down into her gray eyes, wet with tears she wouldn't shed. She was right. What I'd done to her just now wasn't something I'd do to one of my lowest whores. But goddammit. This woman was mine. MINE! And no, I didn't feel the least bit guilty for proving that to her. "Yes, I do," I told her.

My honesty took her by surprise, and she stiffened in my arms as she stared at me. She jerked her eyes away and changed the subject. "I'd like to continue the self-defense stuff with Enzo."

A gruff laugh escaped. "So you can take me down and escape?"

"Yes." There wasn't an ounce of humor in her voice.

I studied her. She was perfectly serious. "If you want to learn how to beat me in a fight, then you'll train with me." I trusted Enzo with my life, and Veda's, but there was no fucking way anyone else was laying a hand on her from now on except for me.

"I'd rather train with Enzo."

"No."

She weighed my response and decided not to fight me. At least not now. "I'd like to get the rest of my stuff from my apartment. If they haven't evicted me yet and thrown it all away."

"You haven't been evicted. Tristan found out where you lived the day we found out who you really were and I've been paying your rent."

Her head snapped around to look at me, her expression shocked. "You have?"

"Of course." I didn't know why that came as such a surprise. The monthly amount was minuscule, and I barely noticed it coming out of my account.

"Thank you," she told me.

Her gratitude was genuine, and it made me uncomfortable after what I'd just done. "It's nothing. I'll send a couple of my men to collect your things."

"I want to go myself."

"No." My answer was swift and final.

I felt her stiffen just before she jumped out of my lap and swung around to face me. "You *can't* just keep me locked away like a bird in a cage!"

"I can. And I will."

The tears that had threatened finally overflowed to run down her cheeks. If she noticed them, she didn't show it. Her hands fisted at her sides. "Luca. You can't."

I sat up in my chair, my elbows on the arms, and pressed the tips of my fingers together. Tilting my head to the side in a silent question, I waited for her to realize I would do whatever the fuck I wanted, especially in my own home. And what I wanted was for her to stay here, with me, where no one else would ever touch her again.

She took a breath and regrouped. "Luca, please. I've been locked up in your house for weeks."

I raised one eyebrow.

"Look," she said, her voice carefully level. "I know you have good intentions, and I'm not completely stupid. If you say I'd be in danger on my own, then I believe you. I mean, it makes sense. But..." She looked around as if she'd find the words she was trying to say on the floor, or perhaps the walls. "Luca," she finally said, her eyes pleading with me to see her side of it. "What kind of life will that be for me? My entire life will pass me by with me locked up here until what? Until you tire of me and don't give a shit anymore? Until you die? Then what'll happen to me?"

The way I felt right now, with my body already hardening for her again, I didn't see myself ever tiring of her. Dying, on the other hand...there wasn't any avoiding that. "I'll make arrangements to make sure you're taken care of."

"So I'm just supposed to wander around this house like a ghost? Luca...I'd go insane."

I stared up at her as she stood there, arms akimbo and pleading gray eyes luminous with her tears. If I had my choice, I would lock her away in my bedroom and never let her step foot outside of it. Not even to the balcony to get some sun. But I had to admit to myself that perhaps she was right. It wouldn't be healthy for her. And maybe we could find some sort of middle ground. "Let me think about it."

She looked like she wanted to say more, but in the end, she just nodded. "Okay. Thanks."

I gave her a nod and stood. "I'll get with my men about going to get your things. What we can't find room for here, we can put in storage until you decide what you want to do with it."

"Okay," she said softly. "That would be great."

"Don't look at me like that," I told her quietly. Then I kissed her hard and sent her off, her bare feet silent on the hard floors.

Reaching across my desk, I picked up my cell and called Lisa, who answered on the first ring.

"Yes, sir? Did you need something?'

"Would you please keep an eye on Veda? And call me immediately if she tries to leave the house."

"Of course. And Kevin is about to head out to pick up the things he needs to increase your security system."

"Excellent. Thank you, Lisa."

"Let me know if you need anything else, Mr. Morelli."

"I will." Ending the call, I texted Enzo. We had a lot to do to before my meeting with my father tomorrow.

CHAPTER 15

LUCA

"You need to let that woman go. Your plan failed. She's no use to you anymore."

"Veda is none of your concern, *padre*."

"How many times do I need to tell you. Luca? Eh? She's a distraction—"

We'd been going round and round with this same conversation for the past hour. "She will be DEAD if she leaves my house! Or worse! I'm not throwing her out to the wolves who are constantly prowling around just waiting for their chance to take me down!" What I'd told Veda earlier was true. My family had enemies, and they were constantly looking for a weak link. Some way to break us apart. And I was quite certain, by now, word about Veda had gotten out. If anyone managed to get their hands on her...

I couldn't even think it.

At my outburst, Luigi Morelli leaned back in the dark leather throne he used for a desk chair and leveled his steady gaze at me, but I refused to squirm beneath it like I did when I was a child. As a matter of fact, it'd been many years since I'd felt so intimidated by my father.

"She's a weakness, Luca," he repeated. "Just like Maria was. And look what happened then. Your relationship with her lost us thousands of dollars because you made the mistake of trusting her and her brother. At least Mario had the intelligence to see it for what it was and try to do something about it."

I laughed, long and hard. "Are you trying to make me believe that his killing Maria was his way of trying to *help* me? To help the family? Is that the bullshit reason he gave you?" My amusement faded fast. "What Mario did was the act of a rat. Family or not, he should've been taken care of years ago."

"He saved us from more bad business dealings with that family."

"He went to the Feds. He went into witness protection. God only knows how much he told them about us. How was that saving this family?"

"That was just an act to throw the Mexicans off. So they would continue to trust us. Continue to trust you."

An uneasy feeling wrapped itself around me. "What exactly are you saying?

"I'm saying that woman you claim loved you so much was taking more than her share of the deal and she was distracting you with her tits and her cunt while her men shorted us in product and still took their full share of the money."

It was suddenly too hot in the room and my lungs couldn't take in enough air, but I wouldn't give him the satisfaction of seeing my reaction. "You're lying. Maria wouldn't have done that. This was all Mario telling you this shit as an excuse to do what he did because he knew you'd fucking believe it. Just like you always believe his bullshit."

My father put his elbows on his desk, lacing his fingers together as his face took on an expression of fatherly concern. One I knew for a fact was nothing but a facade to get information. "Why do you hate your brother so much, Luca? Huh?"

"What the fuck kind of question is that? *He murdered the woman I was going to marry.*"

"Ah..." He waved his hand in the air, his expression sour like something stank. "All dealings aside, that marriage would've never worked, and you know it. The only thing those spicks are good for is fattening my gut with their spicy food and cutting my grass."

My blood boiled at the derogatory term, but I knew better than to try to correct him. The last time I'd tried, he'd backhanded me so hard my teeth had ached for a week, and, more importantly, he'd cut me out of the next deal. I'd lost a lot of money because of it. The bastard. Besides, it wasn't true. I've never had a bad dealing with the cartel. People who didn't know me from Adam had more honor and loyalty than my own fucking family, as long as you followed the rules. And the main reason for that was this man sitting directly across from me. So it wasn't worth my time to argue with him.

And yet...something deep down inside of me had to ask, "Why do you still prefer him?"

"Luca, you know that isn't true..."

"I've been here," I told him. "I'm the one who's here running our business, doing our deals, protecting our family, while that fucker is off taking a fucking vacation with the Feds. And you"—I pointed my finger at him—"you protect him. Every fucking time. Why, *padre*?"

"Mario is my oldest son. My firstborn. Nothing he's done will change that." He sighed at my expression of disbelief. "Luca, you've known your entire life what that meant for you. Your position in the family right now is only temporary."

"So you can replace me with that rat of a brother?"

He slammed his hands down on his desk. "Enough! Mario is not a rat! Your *fratello* has made sacrifices for this family. Many sacrifices! Things you don't understand."

This was the first time in a long time we'd spoken so openly. "And I haven't made sacrifices?" I asked him in disbelief. "I haven't been here for the family? I haven't taken hits? All in the name of saving the face of this *family?*"

"Your brother has what it takes to run this business when I'm gone—"

Fury brought me to my feet. "My brother is a fucking COWARD!" I put my hands on the edge of his desk and met his eyes, so similar to my own. "He goes after women instead of coming for me himself. And you know why, *padre?* Because he's weak. Because he doesn't have the balls to take me out. Not since we were teenagers, when I began to realize who he really was, and I started working independently to find my place in this family instead of just being Mario's baby brother." I pushed off the desk and straightened my suit jacket, preparing to leave. "I don't know why I bother. You don't hear a fucking word I say."

He was unaffected by my sudden temper. "Luca, you're being overdramatic. You act like your brother has some kind of special target on you. Like he's jealous of you or something." He laughed like that was the most hilarious fucking thing he'd ever heard. When I didn't share his humor, he sobered and gave me a long look before he sighed. "All right, all right. Keep the woman if you want. Use her if it helps keep that damn temper of yours in check. Fuck her until her pussy is worn out and then find a new pet. But don't let that cunt get under your skin. That's your problem, Luca. Under that tough exterior of yours, you're just a romantic at heart. Just like your mother." I half expected him to pat me on the head like a child, and maybe he would have if I was closer.

I realized then that talking to him like this was a waste of my time. My father would always view me as the younger son, a good errand boy, but not worthy of anything important. The second in line for the throne. One who will never have the chance to wear the crown and so is only tolerated, just in case, but never expected to really do anything of importance.

But I knew things that even my father didn't. I wasn't as stupid as he thought. "What Mario told you about Maria was a lie. She never stole from us, and neither did any of her men. But you'll never believe that. You'll never believe me. Believe *in* me. So I think we can stop pretending that I matter to you at all. I was a fool to ever think otherwise." Taking the cash from my pocket that was his cut of the money I'd laundered through my clubs, I slammed it down on his desk, turned, and walked out, shutting the door behind me.

He didn't try to call me back.

CHAPTER 16
VEDA

L uca had been gone all morning, leaving me to wander around the house. I'd joined Lisa in the kitchen while I had a cup of coffee, but she had other things to do than entertain me, so I was once again on my own.

I didn't like being on my own. It gave me too much time to think. Surprisingly, Luca had never come to bed last night. But instead of enjoying the time to myself, I found myself tossing and turning, unable to fall asleep until the early morning hours when I finally dozed off from pure exhaustion. I'd woken up a few hours later, bleary-eyed and more tired than when I'd gone to bed.

Upstairs, I found a pair of yoga pants and some sneakers and then rummaged around in Luca's drawers until I found a T-shirt I didn't think he'd mind me borrowing. And if he did, well, then maybe he shouldn't lock me in his house under guard after he jizzed all over me with nothing to do but go through his stuff.

As I made my way down the stairs, I overheard Enzo talking to someone near the front door. The words "apartment" and "truck" caught my attention. Were they talking about *my* apartment? Getting my stuff? My stomach flipped with excitement at the prospect of packing and moving, which only proved how completely desperate I was to have something else to occupy my mind.

Hurrying now, I caught them as they were about to walk out the front door. Both were casually dressed in jeans and T-shirts, which got my hopes up even more. "Hey! Where are you going?" I called out.

Enzo and the guy with him stopped. The new guy checked me out from head to toe, the expression of surprise on his ruddy face almost comical. Enzo indicated for him to wait. "We're about to head over to your place and get your things," he told me. "Tristan will stay here in the house with you."

"I wanna go, too," I blurted.

Enzo tilted his head as he studied me. His eyes dropped to what I was wearing, much like his friend's had. "I think we can handle it."

"But you don't even know what I want and don't want." I was desperate to get out of this damn house and grasping at straws, I knew, but I had to try. "Come on. I'll be with you. It'll be perfectly safe. I promise won't try anything."

"No." Grabbing the door handle, he opened it, letting the other guy out.

I grabbed his arm, feeling his muscles tense for a moment before they relaxed again. "Call Luca and just ask him. Please?" As soon as the words were out of my mouth, I could've kicked myself. There was no way in hell Luca would let me go. But there was also no way Enzo would take me without his permission, so it was the only chance I had, albeit a very small one.

With a heavy sigh, Enzo pulled out his phone and tapped the screen before putting it up to his ear.

I crossed my arms over my chest and shifted my weight from side to side as the phone rang. And rang. And rang.

"He's not answering," Enzo told me as he put his cell back in his pocket. "I'm sorry, Veda. But you're going to have to stay here."

"Enzo, please. I have to get out of this house." And if I was going to do it, I knew this was going to be my only chance until Luca deemed it safe enough to take me out himself. "Please," I repeated. "I don't have that much stuff. It'll be a quick trip and I can help."

"Veda. I said no."

An idea came to me. "But, I have stuff I don't want you to see." I ducked my head like I was embarrassed. "Private things."

One eyebrow lifted. "I promise you your 'private things' aren't anything I haven't seen before."

Stamping my foot on the floor like a child, I tried one last time. "Enzo, come on! I'll be perfectly safe. I'll hide on the floor of the truck. I'll let you sneak me in the back way. I need to get the fuck out of this house. And I'll take full responsibility with Luca."

I couldn't see enough of his expression with his sunglasses covering his eyes, so I thought I'd lost my argument when he opened the door. But he only yelled that he would be right out and then closed it again. Pulling his cell back out of his pocket, he tapped the screen again, and I heard a phone ringing. This time it was picked up, and I heard Luca's voice on the other end.

Well, hell. There went my chances of getting out of the house. Dammit.

"Luca. I'm sorry to bother you. We're about to head to Veda's place to get her things and she would like to come with us."

I had no hope at all that he would say it was okay, yet I still waited, wishing for a miracle.

"I can bring Tristan and leave someone else here at the house." A pause. "Yes." Another pause. "Yes. I understand. Okay. We'll be back in two hours. No more." He tapped the screen to hang up the call and shoved the phone back into his pocket. "Okay," he told me. "Let's go."

"He's letting me go?" My mouth dropped open. I couldn't believe it.

"Yes," Enzo said. "But he's not fucking happy about it, so let's go before he changes his mind. He swore to string me up by my balls if we're not back on time."

He didn't seem that concerned about Luca's threat, but he didn't need to tell me twice.

Enzo opened the door again, and I walked out into the sunshine with a grin on my face. I couldn't believe I was getting to go back and see my home of the last five years. Perhaps for the last time.

"Wow. You weren't kidding when you said you didn't have a lot of stuff."

I looked around my apartment. It seemed so tiny to me now, even though it was an older building so it was over 700 square feet, which was big for a one-bedroom apartment in Austin. Enzo had had the key. Apparently, I wasn't even to be trusted with letting myself into my own home. "Yeah, well, my sister didn't pay me enough to own a fancy lake house. And I was really only here to sleep most of the time. And that was only when Nicole wasn't having some kind of dramatic crisis because she got turned down for a part or something. At least until recently."

It just occurred to me that the last few months before her death, she'd been slowly but surely not needing me as much. Little by little, I'd had more time to myself. And now I knew why—because she was dating Mario. And me, well, I'd just been so damn happy to have a little freedom, I never questioned why.

"So let's get going," Enzo told the three guys who had followed us over in the moving truck. "Veda, is there any furniture here you don't want?"

"Um…" I looked around. My decor was what one would call "shabby chic meets whatever I could find at Goodwill." The walls and rug were the standard apartment beige, my couch was bright pink, my walls were covered with tapestries of misty mountains and sunlit forests I'd never get to see, and my small television was using bright green milk crates as a stand. They also doubled as my bookshelf and were filled to overflowing with the paperbacks I grabbed every time I went to the thrift store and never had time to read.

Right off the living room was a small galley kitchen that had a breakfast nook at one end, aka the plant room. Except they were fake plants because I didn't have time to keep real ones alive. In the kitchen was a microwave, a few pots and pans, and a set of dishes Nicole was going to throw away a few years before during one of her home cleanses. I didn't particularly like the design, but at least I didn't have to eat off of paper plates.

My bedroom was off to the left, with a bathroom right outside of it. I actually did like my bed. It was made of gray-washed wood with a matching dresser and had been a gift from my dad when I'd first gotten this place. It kind of reminded me of what you'd find in a rental on the coast. But the mattress was getting worn and there was no room in Luca's house for another bed.

So that left my clothes and other personal stuff. "I want to keep the couch, the TV, and the bedroom set, but not the mattress. If that can go into storage maybe?" I looked to Enzo for confirmation, and he nodded. "I'll take the tapestries and my books and photos back to Luca's, along with my clothes and other personal stuff."

Enzo snapped his fingers. "You heard the lady. Start packing everything up. The things she wants in storage, we'll put in the back of the truck and you guys can take it there after we drop her back off at the house."

One of the guys started taping up boxes to use and I grabbed a couple and took them into the bedroom with me to start boxing up my clothes and shoes.

I was on the floor in my closet, separating my clothes into what I wanted to keep and what I didn't, when the ruddy-faced dude who'd been with Enzo in the house earlier stepped inside and closed the door behind him.

My head snapped up. "What—"

I was cut off when he dropped down onto his haunches and pulled a small gun out of the back of his pants and aimed it at my face. "Shut your mouth or I'll put so many holes in that pretty face of yours, no one will be able to identify you."

My jaw snapped shut.

"What do you know about the deal Luca has going down at the end of the month?"

I stared at him like he'd lost his fucking mind, but managed to keep my voice down. "I don't know anything."

"Ah, come on, honey. You can do better than that. What will Mario say when I tell him you're not coming through for him?"

I stared at him, uncomprehending for a moment. And then I started to shake. I couldn't stop it. It started at my hands and moved up through my arms until it fanned out across my torso. My teeth chattered and my bowels twisted in fear. For some stupid reason, I'd believed that once I got back to Luca's no one would be able to get to me. "I told Mario. Lu...Luca doesn't share any of that with me."

"Of course he doesn't. He's not fucking stupid. But come on, Veda. You're a smart girl. You'll figure something out." Still aiming the gun at the center of my forehead, he picked up a black, lacy tank that I usually wore under one of my low-cut shirts and brought it to his face. He inhaled deeply, his deep-set, brown eyes never leaving my face, then dropped it on the floor and grabbed his crotch, obviously adjusting himself in his jeans. "The next time I find you, you'd better have something for me. Or do I need to remind you about the deal you made?"

I shook my head with jerky movements.

Standing up, he shoved the gun back into the waistband of his pants, put his finger to his lips, and opened the door, listening for a second before stepping out. As soon as he was gone, I surged forward and shut it behind him, then backed into the farthest corner and pulled my knees up to my mutilated chest, which suddenly throbbed in pain.

Jesus, how could I have thought he'd forget about me?

The only reason I was still alive right now was because I'd made a deal with Mario the same day he'd dumped me in the woods. Terrified he would kill me, I became desperate. So when he offered me a way to be useful to him, I took it. I didn't even think about it. Anything to get the hell away from him and his manic mood swings that flew back and forth between fits of rage and sobbing confessions and everything in between.

So I agreed to be his spy. Any and all information I saw or overheard was to be reported directly to him through one of his men who would be in contact with me.

His men were everywhere, he'd assured me, and they would find me.

I was to tell them what I knew, and they would report back to Mario. However, I'd foolishly assumed that Luca's security was locked down tight and that his men were loyal. I'd assumed that Mario was out of his mind, and that once I got away from him, I would be safe.

Oh, god. I needed to tell Luca what was going on. *No, no. I can't.* Slapping my hands over my face, I squeezed my eyes shut, remembering what I'd agreed to, and what the consequences would be if I snitched.

Mario, the bastard, was smarter than I'd given him credit for.

He'd sworn to me that if I *forgot*, and *happened* to let anything slip to Luca about any of this, he wouldn't kill *me*. Oh, no. That would be too easy. In the short time we'd been together, Mario had gleaned quite a bit about me. Like how, for the majority of time I'd been with him, all I'd really wanted was to die. To remove myself from their game. To no longer be a piece on the board.

So, no. That move was too easy.

He wouldn't come after me...he would kill my parents.

He would kill Luca.

And despite everything, I knew I wouldn't be able to live with myself if that happened. I wanted to get away from him, yes, because I knew this life wasn't something I could ever accept. Because I hated him just as much as I craved him. But live in a world without him in it?

I didn't think I could do it, especially knowing I was the reason he was no longer there. I wouldn't be able to live with myself knowing I had purposefully caused someone else's death.

My breath caught on a sob, and I moved my hand over my mouth to stifle it. I couldn't let anyone hear me. If they did, Enzo would be here in a flash, demanding to know what was going on. I didn't know how long I'd be able to hide in this closet before he came looking for me anyway. Of course, I could always tell him I'd just gotten overwhelmed about leaving the only home I'd known for all of my adult life. Or I could tell him I was on my period. Or both. That should shut him up pretty quick.

But the shaking. I had to stop the shaking.

Taking a breath, and then another, I clambered onto my knees and started going through my clothes again, trying to keep my mind on anything but what had just happened. Hopefully, by the time I came out of this room, Mario's guy would be out in the truck, and I could use the ride home with Enzo to get my shit together before I saw Luca. Because I knew if he saw me like this, if he started demanding what was going on—or worse, showed concern—I would lose it.

I'd completely fucking lose it.

Okay, Veda. Get your shit together.

I finished packing what clothes I wanted, and by the time I pushed the boxes out to the living room, Enzo was sitting on the floor against the wall, waiting for me, one arm on his bent knee as he rubbed the tips of his fingers together. His phone was in his other hand. All of my furniture was gone, and the kitchen cabinets were all open and empty. The only thing that was left out here were my fake plants. Even the trash was gone.

When he saw me, Enzo closed whatever he was looking at on his phone and rose to his feet. "Do you wanna keep those?" he asked, pointing his chin at the plants. His sunglasses were on top of his head, resting in his dark, spiked hair, allowing me to see his eyes. They were haunted by the things he'd seen and done in his life, but not cold. There was a speck of something there. The same something that made him so patient with me when we were training. It was the thing that made me trust him, even though he was just as scary as Luca, if not more so.

I glanced over to the breakfast nook and shook my head. "Um, no. They can go with the other stuff I don't want." I smiled at him, still a bit shaky, but there. "They're not real. I never had the time to keep a plant alive. Or a pet. Even though I've always wanted both."

With a nod of understanding, he walked over and gathered up the plants to take down to the Dumpster. "Let's go, then. I need to get you back. I'll send someone up for one of those boxes."

With one last look around, I picked up the smaller of the two and followed him out to the SUV, carefully keeping my eyes down as he ordered a couple of the others to run back inside for the other box and whatever was left in the closet. Shoving my box into the back seat, I climbed into the passenger side, leaving my door open to let some of the heat out. Not that it was much cooler outside. The summers in Texas were a bitch.

The ride back to the lake house was blessedly silent and cool, thanks to Enzo cranking the AC in the car. As soon as we got there, I grabbed my box, thanked Enzo, and, after he assured me he'd bring up the other larger box personally, I hurried upstairs to Luca's room to unpack and take a shower.

Dropping the box outside of the closet, I locked myself in the bathroom, stripped off my sweaty clothes, and got into the shower.

As soon as the water was on, the dam I'd built up around my emotions burst free. A choked sound escaped. And then another. And then I started crying with great, heaving sobs. Disoriented, I threw out my hands until I hit the tiled wall, wet from the steam of the shower, and put my back to it. My legs gave out, and I slid down to land hard on my ass, my hands coming up to cover my face as fear wracked my body so hard I couldn't breathe.

CHAPTER 17
LUCA

I waited for thirty minutes for Veda to join me for dinner before I drank down the rest of my wine and went looking for her. Setting down my glass, I shoved my chair back, leaving my jacket draped over the back, and stalked up the stairs. I wasn't in the mood for this shit today.

My bedroom door was open and the room was dark.

I was about to go start checking the other bedrooms when I felt a warm breeze brush the back of my neck. Spinning on my heel, I looked again and noticed the patio door was open just wide enough for a smaller person to fit through.

An uneasy feeling trickled down my spine and tightened my balls. "Veda?"

Forcing my legs to move, I walked over to the doors that led out onto the balcony and slid the glass open wide, almost afraid of what I would find.

Veda stood in the corner of the balcony up against the railing, staring out at the lights flickering across the lake. Barefoot, as always, she wore a white sundress with thin straps that left her arms and shoulders bare and fluttered around her knees in the breeze that blew in off the water. With her light hair and pale skin, she was a phantom standing there in the light of the moon. A ghost of something that would always be just out of my grasp.

Chills ran up and down my arms, and my words came out harsher than I intended. "Veda, your dinner is getting cold."

She didn't turn around. Didn't respond.

"Veda," I said, a little louder this time.

Startled, she swung around, her arms slipping from the railing to hang limply at her sides, the top peaks of my brother's initial a deep contrast against her skin.

Even from where I stood, I could see her face was swollen and red. My hand went to the gun in the back of my pants, and I quickly scanned the balcony for whoever the fuck had made her so upset, checking behind me and over the railing, but no one else was there. I let go of the weapon and dropped my arm back to my side. "What's happened?" I asked. She stood so straight, her body so tense, I was afraid to go near her for fear she'd shatter like glass. "Veda? Tell me what happened right fucking now," I commanded.

She blinked a few times, like she was coming out of a daze, and visibly relaxed. Not a lot, but enough that I no longer feared she was about to break apart in front of me. "Nothing," she said quietly. "Nothing happened."

Lies fell out of that pretty mouth as if she believed them. With another glance around, I cautiously approached her. Something was off here; I just couldn't pinpoint what it was. "Why are you lying to me?" I scanned her body, searching for the cause of the tingles crawling down my spine.

Her eyes were glued to my face as I got closer. "I'm not... I'm just...nothing happened. Just clearing out my place today. I don't know. I'm just feeling..."

"What?"

She wrapped her arms around her midsection and shrugged. "I don't know. Things. I'm feeling things about leaving my home."

"Things?" I repeated.

With a big sigh, she turned her back to me and put her arms back up on the railing. "Yeah. Things."

She was feeling *things*.

Fine. Let her feel whatever the fuck she wanted to feel. That didn't mean she could lock herself away up here. "I was waiting for you downstairs at the table."

"I'm not hungry."

"Veda, you have to eat."

Turning her head until she could look at me over her shoulder, she said, "Why? I'm not hungry."

"Because *I* am hungry, and I'd like your company, that's why." I was suddenly angry, my temper on edge after the meeting with my father. I wasn't in the mood for her games tonight. "So come on." Gripping her upper arm, I pulled her away from the view and walked her in front of me back into the bedroom.

But once we were inside and I'd closed the patio door behind me, she yanked her arm from my grip. "I don't need you to lead me around like a child."

"Then stop acting like one!"

A look of disbelief crossed her face. "Just because I'm sad that I was *forced* to move out of my apartment today, *against my will*," she said the words slowly, like I was an idiot who didn't understand plain English, "I'm acting like a child?" She crossed her arms and looked away with a huff before turning back to me. "Am I not allowed to have emotions, Luca? Huh? What the fuck do you want from me? I'm a person. A *person*. I can't just dance around here like one of your whores. Always happy. Never arguing with you. Spreading my legs whenever you snap your fingers."

The image of her willingly spread out on the bed behind her had my cock at immediate attention. "I don't have any whores," I told her evenly. And I never would. I didn't even treat the girls at my clubs like that. I'd grown up watching my father treat women like shit after my mother died. Heard them crying in the kitchen after he'd left. He was a bastard, and I'd sworn I would never treat another human like trash, no matter where they came from.

That brought her up short. "Then who did you fuck before I got here?" She seemed genuinely curious as she waved her hand at the offending piece of furniture behind her. "Do you make a habit out of kidnapping innocent women and forcing them to share your bed?"

"That's none of your concern." The truth was, I didn't. I hadn't. Not that I didn't fuck on occasion. I wasn't a goddamn monk. I just didn't bring them to my home. The number one reason being safety. Mine, and theirs. And the second reason being that I didn't want them here. I've never wanted any woman here.

Not even Maria, if I were to be completely honest with myself. I was going to buy her a house here in the states. One we would share as husband and wife. But this house. This was my refuge. I never wanted anyone else to know about this place besides me and my most trusted men.

Not until this woman/child with hair like summer wheat and a body that drove me fucking insane caught me in her innocent gray eyes.

I wanted her here so fucking badly I forbid her to leave the house. I wanted to protect her. I wanted to watch every expression on her face. Wanted to feel the way she made my blood rise when she stood up to me. And how she made it burn when she was underneath me.

Veda was watching me. Waiting for something. "What?" I snapped.

She shook her head. "Nothing."

Closing the distance between us, I took her jaw in my hand and forced her to meet my eyes. "If you tell me 'nothing' one more fucking time tonight—"

"You'll what?" She stared up at me in challenge.

The corner of my mouth twitched, as did my cock.

"You're going to come eat dinner with me. I'll tie you to your fucking chair if I need to, but you're going to come and sit at the table. With me. And you're going to eat if I have to force it down your throat."

Apparently, whatever had been making her so sad was forgotten. A switch had flipped inside of her, and she gripped my arm and rose up on her toes until her face was as close to mine as she could get it. "Then you better get the fucking rope," she ground out between her teeth.

"I'm warning you, Veda. I'm not in the fucking mood to play tonight."

She bared her teeth at me. "Who's playing? I told you I'm not hungry. I don't want to sit at the table and watch you eat. And I'm not going to willingly go down there just because you fucking demand it."

Releasing her jaw, I bent forward and threw her over my shoulder. As I went down the stairs with Veda trying her best to get me to release her, I bellowed for Tristan who I knew was standing guard by the front door tonight.

He came in as I reached the main room. "I need something to tie her to her chair."

Without a moment's hesitation, he gave me a nod and disappeared back out the door, returning less than a minute later with a handful of silk scarves. I didn't ask him where he'd gotten them. I didn't really care.

Between the two of us, we got Veda secured to her chair in the dining room as she threw herself around like a wild thing and cursed me to hell and back. "Thank you," I told Tristan as I brushed her hair out of her face. Now that she was secured, she'd stopped struggling, glaring at me. "If you think everything is secure, you can go ahead and lock up and take the rest of the night."

"I'll check in with Enzo first."

He left the room without a backward glance. Picking up our plates, I took them into the kitchen and warmed them up in the microwave. The roast would be a little dry, but it was her own fault for refusing to show up to dinner on time.

Setting her plate in front of her, I moved my own meal, so I was sitting directly beside her and could help her eat. Ignoring her death stare, I sat down and unfolded her napkin, placing it in her lap before doing my own. Then I carefully cut off a piece of roast beef and held it up to her mouth.

She turned her head. "I said I'm not hungry."

I set down her fork. "Fine. Then you can sit here and keep me company while I eat."

"I hate you," she hissed.

"Do you, though?" I asked her. "Or do you just hate the fact that I won't allow you to sulk in your room?"

"You didn't care before."

"I care now." Slicing off a good chunk of meat, I stuck it in my mouth. The microwave hadn't completely ruined it. Lisa must've cooked it slowly all day, for it fell apart on my tongue. "Mmmm." I closed my eyes for a moment, enjoying my meal despite the company.

Veda watched me as I picked up the bottle of Shiraz in the center of the table and refilled my glass. Holding it over hers, I asked, "Would you like some?"

She shook her head. She seemed to be resigned to sitting there quietly while I ate.

I set the bottle back on the table and continued eating, one hand wandering over to her thigh, unable to stop myself from touching her. Her skin was so fucking soft as I pushed her dress higher with every stroke until the napkin I'd placed there fell to the hardwood floor. She said not a word, even when I brushed her panties with my fingertips. I loved Veda's legs. They were smooth and firm and shapely, fuller at the thigh, like the sirens of old Hollywood. I loved them even more when they were wrapped around my waist.

My cock thickened as I continued to run my palm up and down her thigh, then letting the tips of my fingers skim around to the inside of her thigh, my very favorite part, where she was so soft and giving, I wanted to sink my teeth into the supple flesh.

I had to use both hands as I finished my meal and picked up my napkin to wipe my mouth. Much as she tried to hide her reaction to me, I heard her sigh of frustration. Saw her chest rising and falling with each rapid breath out of the corner of my eye. She tried to deny it, but she wanted me as much as I wanted her.

Pushing my chair back away from the table, I picked up my glass of wine and leaned back in my chair, settling my gaze on the beautiful woman at my table who still hadn't said a word. "From now on, you will eat dinner with me every night unless I let you know otherwise."

Thunder and lightening clashed in her stormy eyes, and her jaw was tense with anger. "Does it matter at all to you what I want? About anything?"

"No," I told her. But then, out of some sort of masochistic need to have my ego bruised a bit more today, I regarded her curiously. "But if I did, what is it that you would want, Veda? Other than to sacrifice your life by running away, of course."

"I can tell you what I don't want." Gray eyes turned icy cold. "I don't want to sit here with you every night. I also don't want to share a room with you. As a matter of fact,

I'd like it immensely if you'd just stay as far away from me as possible."

Every word hit me like a knife wound, stabbing me over and over, not that I would let her see it. "Is that so?"

"Yes," she gritted out through her bared teeth.

"Hmm." I took a sip of my wine, my eyes never leaving her face, then set my glass on the table. Reaching over, I grabbed her chair and pulled her closer until our knees touched.

Her eyes widened as I started to unbutton my shirt. "What are you doing?"

"Testing your statement."

The ice left her eyes, replaced by caution. "I have to pee."

I laughed. "No, you don't."

"I really do."

"Then go ahead," I challenged her as I reached the last button and threw my shirt open wide as I leaned my elbows on my knees. "I'll buy a new chair. As a matter of fact, I'll buy a whole new fucking dining set. A whole new room, including the floor. Maybe an entire house in another fucking country. A castle where I can lock you away in a tower and fuck you whenever I want."

And where no one can ever hurt you again.

When she saw that wasn't going to work, she tried a different tactic. Gazing at me with pleading eyes, she said quietly, "Luca, please don't do this."

"Do what?" My finger trailed up her bare thigh until I reached the material of her dress and lifted it away, tilting my head so I could see what she was wearing underneath. She tried to close her legs, but Tristan had done an excellent job tying her ankles and her movements were limited. My tongue wet my bottom lip when I saw she was wearing virgin white, just like her dress. Mmmm...a virgin to desecrate. It was a nice fantasy, even though I knew better. I tucked the skirt into the waistband of her panties to keep it out of my way.

"Luca, please..."

I skimmed the pad of my thumb over the thin cotton up the center of her pussy. I could feel the damp heat of her, and all I wanted to do was to take her out of that chair and bend her over the table and shove my cock balls deep inside that sweet cunt.

But that wouldn't prove my point. I needed to hear her say it.

And before this night was over, she would.

CHAPTER 18
VEDA

Luca seemed to be in a particular kind of mood tonight, and it looked like I was going to take the brunt of it, whether I felt like playing or not.

I tried to close my legs, but I could only move them a few inches, not enough to block his sensual touches. Tears of frustration burned the backs of my eyes. My body was already betraying me, so eager to feel his touch. His tongue. His teeth. I barely stopped myself from groaning out loud, my face burning as I admitted to myself that he was right. I was absolutely full of shit. I did want him. And I loved this fucked up shit he did to me.

So, maybe the question I should be asking was, what the hell was the matter with *me*?

I watched the top of his head as he lowered it to my lap, his hair thick and sandy brown, highlighted with bright silver strands above and behind his ears. My thighs tensed in anticipation. But he didn't kiss me, or run his tongue over my sensitive skin. Instead, he pressed his face into the V between my thighs and inhaled deeply. His exhale nothing but a deep rumble that vibrated through my panties and made my insides clench. I closed my eyes, my upper body swaying in my chair as a wave of pure lust washed over me. Maybe he was right. Maybe I should've eaten something, because I felt lightheaded. But deep down, I knew it wouldn't have mattered. That's the way he affected me.

The air conditioner came on, blowing cool air over my overheated skin. Goosebumps danced across my bare shoulders and down my arms as my nipples hardened into tight nubs. I wasn't wearing a bra with this dress as I hadn't expected to go anywhere, and every time I took a breath, pulses of desire shot straight to my groin. I don't know why I'd even put this on. I just hadn't been thinking straight when I'd finished my shower.

Or maybe you'd put it on for him.

Luca lifted his head, moving slowly, like he had all the time in the world to torture me. I felt the heat of his blue eyes like a brand as they roamed over my face, my shoulders, my breasts. He narrowed his eyes when he reached the carving there, and I looked away, not wanting the see the disgust on his face. I wished I'd just thrown on a T-shirt and shorts.

Without warning, he grabbed the thin cotton at the neckline in both hands and yanked hard, ripping my dress right down the middle.

My mouth fell open. "Dammit, Luca! My dress!"

"I'll buy you a new one," he murmured, distracted, his heated gaze on my hardened nipples.

I couldn't cover myself. I couldn't do anything except watch him lift a hand and take one of my nipples between his thumb and forefinger, tweaking it hard enough I gasped as my body surged toward him, silently begging for more. I'd never felt more exposed. Taking my breast in his hand, he squeezed, the pad of his thumb skimming the tip of my tender nipple. "Tell me you don't want me," he said quietly.

My response was immediate, even as I held back a moan. "I don't."

One side of his mouth lifted in a sexy smirk. My heart began to pound as he stood up and kicked his chair away. It crashed into the wall behind him, and I looked around in fear that someone had heard it and would come running in to see what was going on, only to find me half naked and tied to a chair. But no one did.

Luca dropped to his knees in front of me and sat back on his heels. His thigh muscles stretched the black material of his dress pants, and his abs were hard and tight. My eyes went to the small patch of soft, curly hair just slightly darker than his skin that covered the center of his chest. My fingers twitched, remembering the feel of it.

Placing a hand on each of my knees, he ran them up my legs, spreading my thighs as far apart as they would go in the chair. His eyes focused between them, jumping up to my breasts, my hair, and then back down to my pussy. I had to stop myself from lifting my hips when he leaned forward and pressed his lip to the inside of one thigh.

"Do you want me to touch you?" he asked.

"No," I breathed.

"Hmmm," he responded. One hand moved up to my hip, his thumb slipping under the elastic of my panties. He rubbed the crease of my thigh, moving it just slightly inward with every tiny stroke. "Do you want me to touch you here?"

"No." Good god, what was he doing to me?

"I think you do," he told me. "I think you're wet. And aching. I think the only thing you can think of right now is my mouth on your pussy and my cock inside of you. Should I give you that, Veda?"

"No. You're wrong. I don't want you."

Resting his head on my leg, he watched himself as he dipped his thumb between my folds, starting at the bottom and running it up to my clit. My head fell back, and my eyes closed as he circled it once, twice, three times. "I think you're lying," he said softly. "You're fucking soaking wet, Veda. Wet for me."

"It's not for you," I argued, lifting my head. "This is just a physical reaction. You could be anyone touching me. You could be a fucking vibrator."

Pulling my panties aside, his tongue followed the path his thumb had just taken. I wasn't expecting it, and my hips jerked up at the first touch. My womb clenched and released, and a rush of heat made me even wetter. The bastard worked me with his tongue until I couldn't control my own body anymore, my hips trying to press closer to his mouth, my muscles clenching, my body screaming for release. And then suddenly he was gone, and I was left wanting, my womb heavy and aching, my nipples tight and my pussy pulsing. A keening noise came from me before I could stop it.

When I opened my eyes, Luca was still there on the floor in front of me, his hands on his knees. Completely calm, his face expressionless, he watched me as I sat there panting with need like an animal.

A sob burst from me out of nowhere. "Goddammit, Luca! Untie me! Let me go!" From the chair. From his life. From my own life. I was so fucking tired of being played with.

"You don't want me to let you go."

"Yes!" I screamed at him, not caring anymore who might hear me. "Yes, I do!"

Rising up to his knees, he grabbed me by the back of the neck and pulled my face to his. He kissed me hard, thrusting his tongue into my mouth so I could taste myself, taste what he did to me. Releasing me just as fast as he'd grabbed me, he kissed and sucked his way down my throat to my breasts, taking a nipple into his mouth and laving it with his tongue before he nipped it with his teeth. Then he worked his way over to the other one.

My breaths came in gasps, my heart raced, and I writhed on the chair, trying to ease the ache between my legs, the need to come the only thing I could focus on.

"What do you need, Veda?" His breath blew across my wet nipple before he ran his tongue over it again. "Do you need me to touch you here?" He squeezed my other breast. "Or maybe here?" He squeezed my hip, holding me still, his thumb brushing my pussy.

I couldn't answer him. I was too busy biting my own tongue, so I didn't beg him to fuck me. Or at the very least, put his mouth on me again. But somehow, I knew that I wouldn't be satisfied with just that.

I wanted all of him.

He left wet kisses along the inside curve of my breast now, and lower, to my stomach, until my bunched-up dress stopped him. He sank down onto his heels again, both hands on my hips, and nipped at the inside of my thigh, working his way closer and closer to where I needed him to be. "Tell me you want me," he ordered.

"No." The word ended on a moan as he tore the thin strip of material that held my panties up over my hip, then the other side, leaving me open and exposed to his hot gaze.

"Tell me," he ordered. He didn't wait for an answer, and my hips bucked as he put his mouth on me, sucking and licking like he wanted to devour me whole. Like he'd never tasted anything as good as me and never would again.

A needy cry escaped from me as he held me right on the brink of an orgasm, but wouldn't allow me to go over. Instead, he brought me to the edge over and over until I was cursing at him and begging him in equal measures, my muscles trembling and my clit swollen and sensitive.

Finally, he brought me there again. "Yes, Luca, please," I begged him. My blood roared in my ears and my womb clenched hard, the mix of pain and pleasure almost too much to bear. But he pulled away, dropping light kisses on my thighs. "Luca..." His name came out as a hoarse cry. If I could've hit him, I would have.

"What's the matter, *amore*? According to you, I'm just a body. No better or worse than a fucking vibrator," he told me. "So why are you crying my name?"

I stared down at him, my emotions so all over the place I was about to burst into tears again. "What?" I squirmed in the chair as much as I could, trying to ease the needs of my body and not even caring anymore that he saw how desperate I was.

He stood up, pulling out his phone, and my eyes dropped to his cock, thick and hard and straining at the confines of his pants. I wet my lips. But when I looked at his face, his eyes were cold and hard. "Should I call one of my men to finish you off? Tito, maybe? He's quite popular with the ladies, from what I understand." Looking down at his phone, he started tapping at the screen to pull up a number.

"What are you doing?" Horror filled me as he put the phone to his ear. I could hear it ringing.

"I'm testing your theory," he responded. "However, I don't have a vibrator handy. Unless you happened to bring one from your apartment? No?"

"Luca, stop."

He speared me with cold, blue eyes. "Why?"

I just stared at him and pressed my lips together, even though my body was screaming at me to say it! Just say it! But my pride wouldn't let me. Tears welled up and rolled down my face.

"Tell me why, Veda."

"Because..." The phone was still ringing. Maybe he wouldn't pick up.

"Because why?" Cell still to his ear, he shrugged off his shirt, switching hands to get the other sleeve off. My eyes fell back to his cock as he started undoing his pants with one hand. They hung on his lean hips, fly open, when I realized I was leaning forward, my eyes on the head of his cock poking out of the top of his boxer briefs.

"Veda." His voice was low and commanding.

My eyes flicked up to his without conscious thought. I drew back when I saw the turmoil within them through my tears. The anger. The raw need tensing his jaw.

"Tell. Me. Why."

"Because I want you," I whispered.

The cell phone fell to the floor as Luca dropped back down to his haunches and started tugging at the scarves around my ankles as I struggled against the ones binding my wrists. As soon as my legs were free, he undid my wrists and dragged me into his arms as he fell back against the hard floor, taking the brunt of the fall.

"Luca..." My concern was cut short as he took my hips and pulled me up his body until my legs were spread wide on either side of his head. I cried out as soon as his mouth was on me, my orgasm hitting me so hard and fast it knocked the air from my lungs, and I fell forward, barely catching myself on my hands before I bashed my face into the floor.

My head was still spinning when he moved me down his body and then he was inside of me, his cock thick and hard as my body still pulsed around him. Wrapping his arms around me with his hands gripping my shoulders, he bent his knees and jacked his hips, fucking me so hard if he hadn't been holding on, I would've went flying into the wall behind him. I lay across his body, unable to do anything but bury my face in his neck and hang on as he wrapped one hand in my hair and buried himself so deep inside of me, I swear I felt him in my womb. With a shout, his hips bucked, and I felt the warmth of his come with each pulse of his cock.

When it was over, I tried to get up, but he tightened his hold on me. "You're mine," he growled in my ear. "And if you ever let another man lay one fucking finger on you, I'll skin him alive. Do you *comprendere*, Veda?"

"Yes." God, I was a sick, twisted bitch. Because his words brought a little smile to my face. Not that I ever actually wanted someone to get hurt because of me, but just because I'd never had anyone in my life be so possessive over my company. It made me feel wanted. Needed. It made me feel special. And I liked it.

"I'm not fucking around," he warned me. "I will fucking kill him without blinking."

"I know."

He quieted, one hand rubbing circles on my back. "Are you hungry?" he finally asked.

"Yeah."

He sat up, taking my weight with him like it was nothing. His eyes fell to the "M" on my chest, his expression contemplative. Lifting his hand, he traced it with one finger. "This, right here," he said. "This is not my brother's claim. This is for Morelli. *Luca* Morelli. Not Mario." He pressed his lips to the center, then raised his eyes to mine. "Okay?"

"Okay," I whispered.

"Come on. I'll heat up your dinner."

I got to my feet, and he followed. Without even fixing his clothes, he took my plate into the kitchen, and I cleaned up as best I could with my napkin before I fixed my dress and sat down in the chair I'd just been released from, wondering what kind of deal I'd just agreed to with this devil.

CHAPTER 19

LUCA

Days went by and my *vita* and I settled into a routine of sorts. Most mornings she would join me in the gym, usually arriving just as I finished my own workout, and we would go over her self-defense lessons. Although Enzo had warned me, I was surprised by the ferociousness with which she attacked the techniques. And she would be an excellent fighter if she would just get out of her own head, but more times than not, she couldn't believe she could do it, and so she couldn't, even though she insisted on trying over and over until she was so exhausted I brought our lessons to a close and sent her off to get a shower and some food.

In the afternoons—and some evenings—while Veda helped Lisa or read outside on one of the decks, I dealt with my family's business dealings. After my last visit with my father, I knew he would never willingly hand everything over to me. It didn't matter that I was the son who had stayed, the one that put himself at risk so he could remain safe in the confines of his home. It didn't matter what I did, he would never see me as anything other than the baby boy who would help baby birds get back into their nests when they fell, just one action among many that lessened my worth in his eyes. He thought I had no backbone because I treated employees like Lisa with kindness and respect. Because I watched over those who belonged to me. So no, I would never be handed over the position of Boss.

Like everything else in my life when it came to him and the family business, I would have to take it by force.

Dinners, Veda and I spent together. Ever since the night I'd tied her to the chair, she showed up religiously with a smile on her face and an appetite. She seemed content to ramble around the house, and it made me curious to know why she was suddenly so okay with being here when, up until a few days ago, all she could think about was leaving me. It was like once she'd gotten her own stuff out of her apartment, she was more at home here. Or maybe she'd just resigned herself to the fact that this was the way it was going to be from now on.

But who was I trying to fool? In the short time I'd known this woman, "resigned" was not a word I would associate with her. She'd even stopped fighting me about having her own room, and would snuggle into my arms at night like I would be the one to protect her from all the monsters in the world, not knowing that I was one of them. Or maybe she just didn't care anymore.

The monster you know and all of that.

It was strange, and unlike her, and it made me uneasy. Which was why I didn't return her smile when she sat down beside me and smelled the plate of stuffed shells in front of her. "Mmmm." She picked up her fork with one hand and grabbed a piece of garlic bread with the other. "I love Italian food."

I let my eyes travel over her hair, hanging loose over her shoulders the way I liked it. Some of her natural color was coming in at the roots and I made a mental note to have the colorist come back and put it back the way it was. "You've never told me that."

"It's true," she said. "It's my favorite. If it's got tomato sauce and some kind of cheese on it, I'm in. I could eat it every day." Cutting off a piece of the pasta with the edge of her fork, she blew on it before sticking it in her mouth, her eyes practically rolling back in her head. "Oh my god, that's good."

"Lisa is an excellent cook," I confirmed.

"Has she already left for the day?" Veda asked. "I'd love to find out how she makes this sauce."

"She has," I told her. "But I'm sure she'll let you watch her do it next time."

She nodded in agreement, her eyes on her plate. Tonight she was wearing her favorite shirt with the sunflower on the front and a pair of pink knit shorts that hid her gorgeous thighs. It was a while before she noticed I wasn't eating. Fork in one hand and her second piece of garlic bread in the other, she let her arms rest on the table on either side of her plate. "What's wrong?" she asked. "Why aren't you eating?"

I studied her as I took a sip of my wine. "What's going on with you?" I asked her.

Those little wrinkles appeared between her brows. "What do you mean? Nothing's going on."

Nothing, my ass. Although it was nice to have us coexist in the house in peace for once, this wasn't the woman I'd grown to know and…

I shut down that thought before it could complete itself. I didn't love her. I loved to spar with her, verbally and physically. I loved her body. The rare sound of her laughter. Her smile.

Jesus fucking Christ.

I cleared my throat. "I'd like to know why you're suddenly so content, when not a week ago, all you could think about was jumping off one of the balconies and escaping."

She started eating again. "That's not true. I never planned to jump off a balcony. I was going to walk right out the front door." She tilted her head, thinking. "Or maybe wait until we were in the city somewhere and then get lost in the crowd."

"And you no longer have plans to do either of those things?"

Biting off a piece of bread, she wouldn't look at me, but she shook her head. "What's the point?" she said when she'd swallowed and taken a sip of her wine. "You laid down the law that I have to live here, with you."

"I did. But that's never stopped you before."

"Maybe I've had a change of heart," she said, so quietly I almost had to strain to hear her.

"A change of heart," I repeated.

She pointed with her chin at my plate. "Your dinner's getting cold."

"I'll reheat it," I told her. "This conversation is way too good to pass up."

Her shoulders fell and she set down her fork, eyeing the rest of her meal with something akin to sorrow. "Why do you do this?" she asked.

"Do what, *amore?*"

Her eyes met mine. "Ruin my meals."

"I'm not trying to ruin anything. I just want to know why you're not acting like yourself."

"Maybe this is me," she said. "The me I usually am. And the person you've known up until now is just some version of me that you brought out because you were such an asshole."

I had to give it to her, she almost had me with that one. Shaking my head, I said, "No. I don't believe that."

"You don't believe you're an asshole?"

"Oh, I know I'm an asshole. But I don't believe that this version of you is the real Veda. I think the real you is the one I've been dealing with these last weeks. I've felt the fire in your blood. This person"—I waved my hand from her head to her feet and back again—"isn't you. This is someone who's acting like she's content and happy because she's hiding something from me. And it drives me fucking insane when you hide things from me."

"Did you ever think that maybe it's okay if you don't know everything?"

"No," I told her. "Not knowing things is how you get caught with your guard down. It makes me twitchy."

"Well, you have nothing to worry about." She picked up her fork again. "I don't have any nefarious plans to take you out."

I laid my hand on her arm, and her fork clattered to her plate. "*Stop* lying to me."

She stared down at her plate for a long while, and when she finally looked up at me, there were tears in her eyes. "Luca, I'm not hiding anything from you. I'm just trying to make the best out of a bad situation so I can get out of bed in the morning. I'm bored. I'm lonely. And I miss my life. The one I had before. I had friends. Not many, but one or two. I have parents, and I miss them so much I can't stand it. Well, I miss my dad," she corrected.

I sat back in my chair and thought about what she'd just told me. "If I let you call your father, what guarantee would I have that you wouldn't tell him something that would have the cops banging on my door?"

"You wouldn't," she said. "You'd just have to trust me."

I removed my hand from her arm, and she picked up her fork and started eating again, and I did the same. "I'll think about it," I told her after a moment.

She stopped chewing, her eyes flying to my face. "Thank you."

Taking a piece of bread, I said, "Would you like to go out on my boat tomorrow with me?"

Her eyes widened. "You have a boat?"

"Of course, I do. What kind of gangster would I be if I didn't have a way to escape by water?"

It took a second, but then a smile lit up her face. "That's true. At least from what I've seen in the movies."

"So? Do you want to go out on the lake tomorrow?"

"Yeah," she said. "That would be fun." Then, after a minute, she asked, "Do you have water skis? Or like a tube or something?"

I shook my head. "No. It's not that kind of a boat."

"What kind is it?"

"You'll see tomorrow."

Her good mood returned as quickly as it had left, and I smiled as I watched her plow through her dinner with all of the gusto of any Italian worth their salt.

I wasn't going to tell her that tomorrow's excursion was for more than just spending an afternoon on the lake. I didn't want to spoil her joy. It was a simple meeting between families, and I wasn't expecting any problems. I wouldn't have invited her otherwise. However, I would be sure to take the necessary precautions, just in case.

Throughout the rest of the meal, I allowed her to believe she had successfully thrown me off the scent, but I still wasn't fooled. Something more was going on with her. And I was going to find out what it was.

CHAPTER 20
VEDA

Today the temperature outside was going to be in the hundreds, which wasn't unusual for summer in Austin, Texas. But it made me really glad I was going to be spending it on the water. Maybe we could even have dinner on the boat and watch the sun go down. I'd have to ask Luca if that was something that we could do. He'd said it wasn't the kind of boat that pulled a skier behind it, so I assumed it wasn't a speedboat. Although I didn't see what kind of an escape plan it would be if the thing didn't go fast enough to outrun another boat.

In any case, a part of me couldn't wait to get out of this fucking house. And the other part—a much larger part— wanted to hide under the bed until Mario and his men found someone else to play their spy games.

After dinner last night, my nerves were stretched tight. I should've known that my little happy act wouldn't fool a man like Luca. He noticed everything, knew everything that was going on inside his domain. But honestly, I was scared shitless. So far, I'd found out absolutely nothing about any of his dealings, except that he laundered money through his strip clubs. And I only knew that because I'd overheard him talking to Tristan and Enzo in his office the one day I'd gotten up the nerve to eavesdrop. He'd been saying something about how he needed to make an appearance at the clubs so he could check on the girls and make sure everything was running okay.

Something hot and rabid had risen within me at the mention of "the girls," and I'd had to stop myself from storming in there and demanding how exactly he planned to "check on them." Like some kind of jealous girlfriend.

But I wasn't his girlfriend. I was his prisoner.

Walking over to the mirror in the bathroom, I took one last look at myself. My bleached blonde hair with its ashy roots was pulled into two braids that hung over my shoulders, the tips of my hair brushing the tops of my breasts. And I had my favorite swimsuit back, a color-block two-piece in coral pink and lavender. The top—purple on one side and pink on the other—crisscrossed in the front, wrapped around my back, and tied in the front just under my ribs. The lavender bottoms were your usual bikini bottom, with two strips of the pink making up the sides. It was different than the usual Texas stars and stripes everyone else wore, and I loved it.

Or at least, I used to.

Eyeing the bright red scars that now marred my chest, I pulled on a simple black cover up that was basically an oversized T-shirt, slid my feet into my Keds, and went downstairs to wait for Luca to get done with work for the day.

I found Lisa in the kitchen, and was pleasantly surprised to find her packing a large cooler with food and a bottle of wine. She gave me a large smile when I walked in. "You look so cute!"

"Ah, thanks," I told her, glancing down at my white legs. "I can definitely use some vitamin D."

She dismissed my comment with a wave of her hand. "You have gorgeous skin."

My smile trembled a bit at the corners, and I looked away. I didn't want to see the look on her face when she realized what she'd just said.

But instead of being embarrassed, Lisa put down the stuff in her hands, walked over to me, and waited until I met her straightforward gaze. "You have gorgeous skin, Veda. What Mario did...it's temporary. It'll fade away. But do make sure you put some sunblock on."

"I will," I promised her.

"That reminds me," she said. Disappearing into the large pantry, she held up two bottles of sunblock and dropped them next to the cooler, where she had some paper plates and other non-food items in a bag ready to go.

"Thank you," I blurted.

She looked over at me in surprise. "Oh, you don't have to thank me, honey. Mr. Morelli pays me well to pack this cooler."

"That's not what I meant," I told her. "I meant thank you for being a friend to me here."

Putting the last of the items inside, she closed the lid and looked over at me. "We all need a friend sometimes. And it's been my honor to get to know you, Veda."

I blinked against the sudden tears in my eyes. "Same here." We stared at each other for a moment in womanly kinship, and once again I counted my blessings that she put up with a boss like Luca.

"I hope I'm not interrupting."

At the sound of Luca's deep voice, my entire body went on instant alert. I hadn't realized how tuned into him I was until just that very moment. My breathing picked up with my pulse, the fabric of my soft pullover suddenly scratchy against my overly sensitized skin. My breasts felt heavy and a growing ache began in my groin, tightening the muscles low in my belly until I felt a rush of moisture dampening my suit and I could barely resist the urge to squeeze my thighs together. I stared at him, remembering how he'd touched me the night before, and hungering for that touch again.

His blue eyes took in every inch of me, from the top of my braided hair to the soles of my slip-on sneakers, always so intense. He could probably recite to someone exactly what I was wearing six months from now.

Lisa broke the sudden tension in the room. "I packed your dinner, as you requested, Mr. Morelli."

Tearing his eyes away, he gave her an easy smile. "Thank you, Lisa." Then he turned back to me. "Let me get changed and I'll be ready to go."

It was only then I noticed he was still in his black slacks, house shoes, and a dark blue button-down shirt. His top buttons were undone, revealing a swatch of tan skin and soft chest hair, and his jacket was thrown over one arm. "I'll wait here," I told him.

With a smile at Lisa, he left to go get changed.

"Maybe you should follow him," Lisa said from behind me.

I turned back to her, taking a seat at the island. "Huh?"

"Don't act dumb with me," she teased. "Good lord, you two were giving me hot flashes just now."

I didn't even try to deny it. "I don't know what's wrong with me," I whispered.

"I do," she said. "You have the hots for my boss."

"Your boss and my kidnapper," I told her. "Isn't there a name for that. Stockholm syndrome? Is that it?"

"I don't think that's what's happening here." She put the teapot on the stove and turned on the burner. "I think it's more than that. You two have had some kind of current running between you since the moment your eyes met."

"You weren't there when I first saw him. And since you weren't, let me just fill you in. I was drugged and had a hood over my head when I was dropped on *that* couch..." I pointed out the doorway, where we could see the end of the couch in the sitting area near the patio doors. When I turned back to Lisa, she was leaning on the counter with an unreadable expression. "What?" I asked her.

"It's just...I've never seen Luca like this. I mean, he's a passionate man. Anyone can see that. And he has his demons. The way he works. The way he punishes himself in the gym—"

"The way he kidnaps innocent women."

She gave me a disapproving look.

"Don't look at me like that," I told her. "He took me from my sister's home, Lisa. He forced me to stay here, dressed me up like her, and paraded me around the city until his brother was drawn out of hiding. And then he planned to shoot me in front of him."

"But he didn't," she said.

"Really?" I said. "That's your argument?"

"I said he has his demons. I wasn't lying. I've worked here a long time. I've seen and heard a lot of things."

I've seen and heard a lot of things.

Her words ricocheted around my head. Maybe I was going about this whole spying thing all wrong. But my thoughts were interrupted by Luca's return. He strode into the kitchen looking like he was ready to attend a party on a yacht in cocoa brown shorts with big pockets that came to his knees and a white, long-sleeved, pullover shirt made of some thin material you could practically see through. The sleeves were rolled up over his powerful forearms and it was split open from his neck to the tops of his hard abs. On his feet were slip-on sneakers, much like the ones I was wearing, only in brown. The muscles in his arms and back were visible through his shirt as he bent down and picked up the cooler from the floor. "Are you ready?" he asked me.

I had to swallow past my dry throat before I could respond. "Yeah, I'm ready." I hopped off my stool and gave Lisa an awkward wave, then picked up the bag that contained the plates, silverware, and sunblock.

"Be safe," she called after us as I followed Luca out of the room.

Enzo, dressed in light blue board shorts and a black T-shirt, was waiting for us outside, sunglasses firmly in place. As soon as he saw us, he strode forward and took the bag from my hands, taking it to the open back of the SUV. Luca hefted the cooler inside as I got into the backseat and pulled on my seatbelt. "I didn't know Enzo was coming," I told Luca when he got in beside me.

"It's not a good idea to go anywhere on your own when you're in the business I'm in," was the answer he gave me.

"Of course. I just wasn't thinking. I like Enzo." Giving him what I hoped was a carefree smile, I turned to look out the window as Enzo took us down the driveway. But I could feel his eyes on me all the same.

"What's wrong, Veda?"

I opened my mouth to tell him nothing was wrong, but remembering his reaction the last time I did that, I closed it again and shrugged. "I think I've just been in the house too long." As soon as the words were out of my mouth, I winced internally. I wasn't looking to start a fight with him. Not today.

But his response took me by surprise. "I'm sorry. I'll try to arrange it so you can get outside more. And if I don't, and you start feeling too trapped, just give me a reminder. Preferably with your words and not your temper."

My eyes flew to his face, only to find him staring back at me with a teasing smile. Holy Christ, he was a devastating man when he put his mind to it. I blinked a few times, completely forgetting what we'd just been talking about for a few seconds. "No," I said. "I didn't mean it like that."

"But," he paused to make sure he had my attention, "I will not do anything or go anywhere that will put you in danger. Is that understood?" Reaching across the backseat, he took my hand. His thumb gently stroked my knuckles, and I flashed back to the way he'd brushed my clit just like that while I was tied to a chair. My face grew heated, and my inner muscles squeezed tight. I couldn't take my eyes from him.

His blue eyes fell to my mouth, then fell to my breasts, watching them rise and fall with each quick breath as if he knew exactly what I was thinking about. His lips parted and his tongue darted out to wet his bottom lip. And the whole time, his thumb stroked my knuckles.

Enzo's phone buzzed on the seat beside him, reminding me we weren't alone, and I dragged my eyes from Luca as I cleared my throat and looked out the window, forcing those memories out of my head. "Where are we going?"

Luca's voice was low and husky when he answered. "There's a marina a mile from the house. The boat is there."

"But wouldn't that make it hard to escape by water if you needed to?"

Enzo chuckled, and Luca sent him a side-eyed look before answering me. "There are alternate ways to get here if needed."

"Oh." I imagined a narrow path cut into the side of the cliff behind his house where you'd have to hug the rocks, like in the movies, to avoid falling into the lake and possibly smashing your head open on the way.

A few minutes later, we pulled into the marina. Enzo parked the car and picked up his phone while we waited. I knew by now not to just hop out of the vehicle unless we were back at the house.

"All good," Enzo told us after a moment.

"Let's go," Luca said, pulling me by the hand to his side of the car. I slid along the seat and waited for him to get out and scan the area along with Enzo before I took his hand and let him help me out.

A wave of Texas heat hit me, followed by a nice breeze off the water. I put my hand up to shield my eyes from the sun as I looked around. "Wow," I said aloud. There were more boats here than I'd ever seen in one place. Some bigger than other, but every single one of them probably cost a year's worth of rent.

"We're over here."

Luca took my hand and led me down the dock to the left, stopping at something that could only be described as a small yacht. It had to be at least forty feet long and sat high in the water with a covered cockpit. That was about as much as I knew about boats, but it looked as luxurious as they come and I grinned with excitement when Luca jumped on board and held out his hand to me, helping me on before he took the cooler from Enzo. I stood to the side on the back platform as Enzo joined us.

However, my joy was cut short when I started to follow Luca down into the cabin. There, on the white leather benches on either side of a long wooden table, were five more of Luca's men, including Tristan and the one who'd threatened me at my apartment. I froze in the doorway as they all looked at me. "Um, I'm just gonna stay out here," I told Enzo. Quickly, before anyone could say anything, I went back outside and followed the walkway to the front of the boat, where I found more seating around a sunken, square table. Taking a seat, I tried to think of a way to get out of this. I could claim I'd totally forgotten I get seasick. Or I just could say I wasn't feeling good and maybe Enzo would drive me back to the house.

Why the hell did he need so many of his men here, anyway?

"You should put on some sunblock if you're going to be sitting out here in the sun." Luca sat down beside me and handed me a pair of sunglasses, which I took gratefully, hoping they'd hide the fear tearing through me. Then he opened the tube of sunblock, squeezing some in his hand before setting it on the table. "Take off your cover up and turn around," he ordered. "I'll get your back."

But I held up my hand to stop him. "Oh, that's okay. I'm not taking it off."

He was silent for a moment. "Then I'll get the back of your neck."

His tone brooked no argument, so I did as he asked and turned my back to him, pulling my braids out of his way as he began to slather me with sunblock. His strong hand massaged my neck, relieving the tension there.

"What's wrong?" he asked. "And don't fucking tell me nothing."

"I just wasn't expecting so many people," I said. "Actually, I'm not feeling very well. I think I'd rather just go back to the house. I was thinking maybe Enzo could drive me?"

The engine rumbled behind us, and my head snapped up. I needed to get off this boat. I stood up with an, "I'm sorry," and turned to leave, hoping I could jump off before we went anywhere.

But Luca grabbed my hand and pulled me down onto his lap. His arms wrapped around me like two steel bands, holding me there.

"Luca, please. Let me up. I want to get off the boat." Panic surged through me. I couldn't stay here.

"Veda, stop," he barked when I continued to struggle.

The breeze changed direction, and I realized too late that we were already moving. My heart began to pound. "Luca, please. Let me get off." I tried again to get up and got nowhere. It was like trying to struggle my way off of a ride once the bars have locked into place to hold you in. Despite the fresh air, I couldn't breathe, and I stopped struggling as I concentrated on getting air into my lungs.

"Veda." Changing tactics, Luca cupped the right side of my face in his palm and forced me to look at him, his other arm still wrapped around my waist. "*Amore*, what's wrong?" he asked, his tone gentle and his brows lowered with concern. "You were so excited before we got here." When I didn't answer, because I couldn't, he sighed. "I'm meeting someone on the water. That's why I need my men here. It won't take long, but I can't risk my safety. Or yours."

"I thought it was just going to be us." God, I sounded like a whiny teenager. "I'm just not comfortable...god." I pulled my face away from his hand and covered my face. We were out past the buoys now and picking up speed. Maybe if I just stayed where I was, he would stay inside the cabin. The boat was large, but it wasn't that big. The chances of him cornering me by myself here were slim to none. Luca was here with me. And he would have to be there with him whenever they had their meeting.

"Veda, look at me."

Reluctantly, I met his eyes.

He took off his sunglasses, squinting in the sun, and then mine, waiting until my eyes had adjusted to the brightness. "I don't know what's going on with you right now, but I won't let anything happen to you. You have to trust me." He picked up one of my braids and ran it through his fingers. "I should've told you ahead of time that I was mixing business with pleasure, and I apologize. I promise it won't take more than fifteen minutes. Twenty tops. And then we can enjoy our dinner and watch the sunset. All right?"

"All right," I agreed, because really, what choice did I have? I tried to give him a smile, but I could tell he wasn't fooled.

However, after studying me for a moment longer. He wrapped his hand around the back of my neck and pulled me in for a kiss, his mouth gentle and demanding all at once. I let him in, letting his tongue sweep in to taste me as his free hand slid down to possessively cup my ass. When all I could think about was straddling his hips and taking him deep inside of me, he stopped, nipping at my bottom lip before he let me go completely. "How about some wine?" he asked.

"Okay," I whispered, then nodded when I realized he couldn't hear me over the wind.

"Okay," he repeated. With one more kiss, he slid me off his lap and onto the seat, then got up and went to go get our wine, walking more steadily on the water than I did on land.

After he'd left, I picked up my sunglasses where he'd left them on the seat and wiped my eyes before putting them on. I tried hard to get a grip on myself, to forget about Luca's men inside—probably armed to the teeth beneath their lake clothes—and enjoy the sense of freedom that came with speeding across the top of the lake.

CHAPTER 21
LUCA

By the time we'd made our way to a quiet part of the lake, Veda was on her third glass of ice-cold wine and lying across the bench seat with her head in my lap, her earlier trepidation gone. I watched with interest as the wind ruffled the bottom of her cover up, flirting with the tops of her thighs. She was starting to burn, so as much as I enjoyed the view, I tugged it down to cover her.

As Enzo decreased the speed to take us into the cove, she sat up and turned to me with a grin, setting her glass down on the table. It took her a few tries to get it into the holder, and I smiled. "As soon as my meeting is finished, we'll have our dinner."

"That's fine," she told me. "I'm full of this delicious wine right now."

Taking one of her braids, I tugged her in for a kiss. "Stay here. This won't take long."

"Okay."

She looked past me toward the back of the boat, and I knew my men were getting into position. "Veda." I waited until her eyes were on me again. "If anything does happen, I want you to hit the deck and stay down. No matter what you hear. Do you understand? I will get to you."

I couldn't see her eyes behind the sunglasses, but I could see the tension in her shoulders and in the lines around her mouth. Taking her face in my palms, I smiled. "Everything will be fine. This is just a simple meeting. I wouldn't have brought you with me if I thought there was any chance at all of things going south. But it's good to know what to do. Just in case."

"Then why did you have to bring so many men?"

"It never hurts to have a show of force. And also, because I know he will have just as many. I can't let him outnumber me."

"Just in case," she said somberly.

"Just in case," I agreed. Standing up, I dropped a kiss on the top of her head. Her hair was warm from the sun and smelled like coconuts from her shampoo. Picking up the wine bottle, I poured what was left into her glass. "Just relax and enjoy the sun, *amore*. And I'll be right back."

I felt her eyes on my back as I walked past the cabin to the back of the boat, pushing my sunglasses to the top of my head. Gesturing to Enzo to keep an eye on her, I joined Tristan on the back platform while the rest of my men spread out around us and along the side of the boat. Water lapped over the edge and onto my shoes as Gino Ricci and his four sons pulled up slowly alongside us. Unlike the rest of us, Gino was dressed like he'd just walked out of the office in a pinstriped designer suit and patent leather dress shoes. I raised my hand in welcome as their boat lined up with ours, the bows pointing in opposite directions. One of my men and one of his anchored us together with a hand on the railings.

I stepped to the edge and opened my arms, Gino doing the same. Taking his shoulders, I kissed him on both cheeks. "Thank you for coming."

Gino eyed my men. "Such a show for a casual meeting, Luca."

"I need to protect my interests, my friend. I'm sure you understand."

His eyes were drawn to the bow where Veda was waiting for me. "I can see that."

Even standing in the hot Texas sun, my blood burned, and I felt more than saw Tristan take a casual step toward me. I flexed the fingers of one hand, letting him know I had everything under control. I knew bringing her with me would be a distraction. It was one of the reasons I'd invited her. I was hoping by having Veda on board, it would show Gino that what I was about to offer was sincere and not a trick.

"So what is this all about, Luca?" he asked as we separated. "Why are you dragging me out into this god-awful heat when we could be having a perfectly civilized meeting at my office?"

"Let me get you a drink," I offered. "And then we can get down to business."

"Yes, thank you."

I turned to Tristan and gave him a nod and he disappeared into the cabin of the boat, returning a few moments later with a small cooler filled with an assortment of hard liquors on ice, including Gino's favorite limoncello. "I would offer you something to eat, but unfortunately, I'd like to keep this meeting quick. I don't want to take the risk of being seen."

"Next time," Gino told me as Tristan poured his drink and handed it across the water. Then did the same for his sons.

I let them all have a sip of their drinks before I brought up the reason I'd asked him to meet me out here. "What I'm about to tell you must stay between us, Gino. Can I trust you with that?"

"That depends," he told me honestly, which was one of the reasons I had chosen him to help me. The Ricci family was a family of honor, and the closest thing I would get to being able to trust anyone. "What is this about, Luca? And, more importantly, what will I get out of it?"

"When my father retires, or dies, his son will take over his position in the family."

Gino frowned. "Yes. That's the way it usually goes."

"The son my father wants as the next Boss is Mario." I watched his face closely, studying his reaction.

As I'd expected, there was a moment of shock before he carefully schooled his expression again. "I didn't know your brother was back in the picture."

"Yes. He recently came out of hiding," I told him. There was no need to go into any further detail. All of the families were aware of my brother's actions over the past few years.

Gino's mouth twisted in disgust. "Your father was always overly fond of that boy, and I never understood why. First born or not, he always seemed a little fucked up in the head, if you ask me."

"You read him well," I told him. "Mario and I haven't had any kind of a brotherly relationship since we were kids. However, my relationship with him isn't what I wanted to discuss with you today." I paused. Took a breath. I had to handle this just right, or I would lose one of my best possible allies. I decided that being straight up with him would be my best chance. "I believe I'm more qualified to take over the family business."

"I agree," Gino said with no hesitation. "You've basically been doing that for the last few years, anyway. Ever since the incident with the cartel when Mario disappeared."

So my brother shooting my future wife in the head while my cock was inside of her was known as an "incident" now. "Yes," I told him, my expression carefully blank. "At least here in Texas."

He took a sip of his drink and smacked his lips with appreciation. "This is good."

I smiled and gave him a nod.

"So, what is it you're asking of me?"

"I have reason to believe that the only way I'm going to get my father to relinquish control of the business to me is if I force his hand. And to do that, I'm going to need the backing of the other families. Especially yours."

"You want me to take your side against Luigi." Gino wiped his brow with a handkerchief he pulled from his pack pocket. "Get me a chair, would ya?" he asked his closest son. A folding chair was produced, and he lowered his ample weight into it, then took a sip of his drink as he wiped the sweat from his head again. "What you're asking for Luca, is war between the families."

"I'm hoping it won't have to go that far."

"But knowing your father, which I do, it will. Hell, I've known that bastard since we were boys with scraped knees and missing teeth." He took another drink, then another, as he thought over what I'd just told him. "What will I get out of risking my life and the life of my boys?"

"I'll cut you in on the new deal I'm working on with the cartel."

"Drugs?"

"Money laundering."

"From drugs?"

"Is that important?" I told him.

He thought about it for a moment. "No, probably not."

"Maria's brother is my contact there, the woman my brother killed. We've stayed in touch over the years, despite my father demanding otherwise."

"Do you trust him?"

"I do. Implicitly."

"And all I need to do is have your back when you take the family business out from under your father?"

"That's it. And for your loyalty, I'll reward you graciously with a monthly cut of the proceeds from my new arrangement with the cartel. Let's say...fifteen percent."

Predictable as always, Gino told me, "Let me have a moment to discuss this opportunity with my boys, if you will."

"Of course." Turning away, I joined Tristan on the other side of the platform.

"Do you think he'll go for it?" he asked me.

"I do," I told him with more assurance than I felt. "He'd be a fool not to. All I'm asking him to do is stand with me when I dethrone my father. There's very little risk for him and a lot of money to gain."

Always the devil's advocate, he said, "But like he said, he's known your father since they were kids. Will that be enough to make him switch loyalties?"

"I guess we'll find out."

"He's ready," Tristan said with a nod over my shoulder.

I walked back as Gino's sons returned to their places around him, and waited to hear his demands. Because, like any good businessman, Gino was fond of negotiating.

"Before I turn on one of my oldest friends," he said with a grave expression. "I have a request."

I gave him a nod, indicating for him to continue.

"I want twenty percent of the profit from the money laundering scam."

This, too, I was expecting. "I can do that, for you, Gino. But please don't let it get around or everyone will start thinking I'm soft." I smiled at him, and he laughed.

Waving his hand in the air, he dismissed the idea. "Of course I would never do any such thing. The business that happens between us is private."

"Thank you," I told him, knowing that he would be good on his word. But as I stepped forward to shake his hand and seal the deal, he held up one finger, stopping me.

"I also want her." His eyes drifted down the boat to Veda.

Taken off guard, my skin crawled with unease. But then I laughed it off, honestly thinking he was joking. "She's not on the table, Gino. Besides, what would your Annie think if you brought another woman home? You'd wake up tomorrow with your balls in a jar on the nightstand." Gino had been with the same woman for over twenty-three years. He'd met her when he first came to Texas, and she was a good southern girl who could cook a brisket like nobody's business and had him tied firmly to her apron strings. No one knew why he'd never married her.

A look of disgust twisted his features. "Eh, I got rid of that whore. I found her fucking one of the delivery guys on my kitchen counter last week."

"Got rid of her" could mean many things, but in our world, it usually meant only one thing. "My condolences, Gino." Despite my sincere tone, my muscles tensed. This wasn't good. I'd brought Veda along because I thought he was still tied up with Annie. And as she wasn't my wife, that meant she was fair game. However, there was no fucking way in hell I would turn her over to someone like Gino, or anyone else for that matter. "But as I said, that one"—I tilted my head toward the front of the boat without taking my eyes from him—"isn't on the table."

The thing with Gino was, even though he was a good, honorable man who I respected, he wanted what he wanted. And once he set his mind on something, he pursued it like a bulldog after a bone until he had it. So, when I saw him get that look on his face, the one that told me I'd been a fucking *stolto* not to have her go below while we carried out our business, I could've kicked myself.

"How about you come to one of my clubs instead?" I offered. "As my guest. The girls will treat you really good, and they'll help you forget all about that unfortunate business with Annie. And every single one of them would be honored if they happened to catch more than your passing interest." I wasn't lying. One of the reasons they chose my club to dance in was in the hopes of becoming a permanent companion of my clientele. They didn't give a shit how we made our money, as long as they got to spend it on expensive clothes and fancy dinners.

"No offense, Luca, but I'm not looking for another whore. I'm looking for a girl just like that." Again, he nodded toward the front of the boat. "Why don't you bring her back here and introduce us?"

I barely refrained from launching myself across the water. "You don't want her, Gino." The more I denied him, the more his interest would be piqued, but I wasn't about to hand Veda, my *vita*, over to this guy. I didn't give a fuck who he was.

Never taking his eyes from her, he finished off his drink and stood, handing the empty bottle to one of his sons before he turned back to me. "Then I think our business here is done. It was good to see you, Luca. Give your father my regards."

"Luca." Tristan stepped up beside me.

I cursed under my breath. "Gino, wait. You don't understand." When he turned back to me, I held up my hand. "Let me get her." I waited until he nodded his agreement. Ignoring the look of triumph he couldn't quite hide, I turned to go get Veda, telling Tristan, "Make sure he doesn't go anywhere," as I passed him.

"Veda." She was where I'd left her, only her feet were on the sunken bench and her ass was on the deck. Her empty wine glass was in the holder on the table. She was leaning back on her arms and had her face turned up to the sun, her breasts thrust up in full view of Gino and his sons. I wanted to rage at her for showing off like that, but I forced myself to get it under control.

At the sound of my voice, she lifted her head. "Hey. Is your meeting over?"

I could tell by the slight slur of her words that she was feeling no pain, which was probably why she was baking in the hot Texas sun without complaint. "I need you to come with me."

She stared at me a moment, then looked back over her shoulder to Gino's boat, still sitting near ours. "Why?" she asked. "Why aren't they leaving?"

"Just do as I say. Please," I added quietly.

After a pause, she climbed down from her spot and walked over to me, bracing herself against the slight rocking of the boat with a hand on the table.

When she reached me, I took her arm and leaned down to her speak in her ear. "Do exactly as I tell you and don't say a word. Not one fucking word. Do you *comprendere?*"

She nodded, her head down and eyes hidden behind her sunglasses, and allowed me to walk her to the back of the boat.

"Gino," I said. "This is Veda." I intentionally left out her last name. I didn't know if he knew of my brother's dead fiancée, but I wasn't about to offer up the information.

He stood from the chair he'd once again claimed and walked as close as he could to the edge. "Veda, what a pretty name. I was just telling Luca how rude he was being by not introducing us."

As instructed, she didn't say a word.

"Veda is not on the table," I repeated, holding up my hand when Gino's angry gaze swung my way. My muscles began to ache with the effort it was taking for me to appear relaxed. "Let me explain, and then I'm sure we can work something else out."

Crossing his arms over his barrel chest, he stared at me while he decided whether to give me the chance or not. "Well?" he finally said. "Go on, then. Explain."

Giving him a nod, I turned to Veda. "Take off your cover up."

Her eyes swung to mine behind her sunglasses. "What? No."

"Take it off now," I ordered.

I saw the tension in her jaw and the way her hands trembled—With fear? With rage?—as she pulled out first one arm and then the other before lifting it over her head and letting her arms fall back to her sides, her cover up bunched in one hand. Her chin lifted in a defiant move, and she wouldn't look at me as she focused on Gino. "*As I said*, the pleasure of Veda's company is not an option. She's Mario's, and I need her." Seething with rage that I was forced to do this, my body nearly vibrated with the need to hide her away from the shocked gazes all trained on the "M" carved into her chest. I hated that I had to cause her such embarrassment, but there was no other way around it.

"Jesus, Mary, and Joseph." Even Gino couldn't believe what he was looking at. "What did she do to deserve that?"

I bristled at how he talked about her like she wasn't standing right there in front of him. "She did nothing to deserve this," I answered truthfully. "But this only goes to prove to you that my brother is an extremely fucked up individual. And therefore, he's not the person we want running this family."

Gino's eyes lingered on Veda's chest, then wandered down to her nipples and stomach and lower. I took a step toward him, my hand going into my pocket for my knife so I could cut them from his head. Only Tristan's hand on my shoulder brought me back to myself. Taking a few deep breaths, I managed to lower the heat in my blood to a simmer. "Are we done here?" I asked him.

His eyes wandered back up her body, and he shook his head with regret. "You're right. I don't want a secondhand whore, especially not one who has a reminder scarred into her skin." His eyes wandered over once more. "It's a damn shame." Dismissing her, he turned to me. "Twenty percent. And you can have my boys as guests at your club."

I stepped forward, my hand extended, just wanting to get him the hell out of here before I did something stupid. "I hope you'll join them anyway," I told him as he shook it.

"Maybe. Maybe. We'll see." We both stepped back as our men released our boats and started the motors. With a wave, I watched them pull away as we idled where we were. Closing my eyes, I took a deep breath.

Without a word, Veda kicked off her shoes and dropped her cover up. Before I knew what she was about, she launched herself into the water just as the boat began to move.

"Veda!" I yelled as she went under.

She popped up out of the water and started swimming toward the shore, her sunglasses floating behind her.

"God fucking dammit." Shucking off my shoes and shirt, I yelled for Enzo to wait and dove into the lake after her. Swimming with long strokes, I caught up to her easily.

"Let me go!" she screamed when I reached her.

"Stop!" I yelled. "Where the fuck are you going?"

"Fuck off!" The bottom of her foot hit me in the chest as she kicked away from me.

I was on her again before she got very far. Grabbing her ankle, I pulled her toward me. Her face went underwater, and she came up sputtering and coughing. Wrapping one arm around her chest, I began to haul her back to the boat. "What the fuck are you doing?" I raged at her.

"Getting away from you!" she yelled back as she started to fight me again.

But we were already at the boat and Tristan was there to take her from me and haul her onto the platform. For the first time, I noticed what she was wearing as I lifted myself out of the water. Or rather, what little she was wearing. I got to my feet as an animalistic growl began deep in my chest when I saw my friend's hands on her bare skin. "Let her go," I gritted out between my teeth.

Knowing I was hanging onto my temper by a thread, Tristan dropped his hands immediately and she stumbled forward into my chest. I grabbed her arm and hauled her toward the cabin. "Go!" I told Enzo as we passed him. "Straight back to the dock. And keep everyone else the fuck out."

"Got it," he told me as the boat picked up speed.

Veda yanked her arm out of my hand as soon as we got below, and I let her. She spun toward me, her gray eyes dark with fury. "You were going to give me to that man!"

"No, I wasn't."

"You were! I was there! He called me a whore…" Her voice broke.

Closing the distance between us, I grabbed her chin and pulled her face up to mine. "No one touches you but me. You're MINE, Veda."

But she shook her head. "You were bargaining me like a piece of property." But some of the venom had left her voice.

"You're mine," I told her again. "And why the fuck are you wearing something like this in front of my men? Do you *want* me to have to kill someone?"

Her eyes widened in disbelief, and she pulled away from me. "It's a bathing suit! What the hell did you expect me to wear on the lake?"

I knew she was right, but logic didn't matter to me right now. The only thing I could think of was that every single man on my boat, and Gino's, had seen way too fucking much of her gorgeous body. Every single one of them would probably be jacking off to her tonight.

I bared my teeth. "You're strutting around looking like that in front of my men! In front of Gino and his sons! Were you showing off out there when I couldn't see you? Was that why he was suddenly so interested in you?"

She stared at me in disbelief. "Oh," she huffed. "Fuck *you*, Luca." She shook her head, her mouth twisted in disgust. "I had no idea this little outing was going to involve so many fucking people, and you know it. Don't you dare try to turn this around on me!"

My blood rushed through my veins and my cock swelled until it was painfully hard. "I'll do whatever I fucking want to you, Veda."

CHAPTER 22
VEDA

He stalked toward me, as graceful and powerful as a big cat, his blue eyes lit with a possessive light and trained on me.

"No," I told him. "Stay away from me. I don't want anything to do with you." I was so fucking angry with him right now I could spit.

"Well, that's too fucking bad," he said, his voice low and husky. "Because you're not getting rid of me, Veda."

I backed away as he prowled after me, taking his time, until my legs hit the back of something. A glance over my shoulder told me it was a bed, large enough for two people to sleep comfortably. Putting out my hand, I tried to stop him from getting any closer. "I'm covered in lake water."

"I don't care."

I could scream, but I knew no one would help me. He could pull out a knife, hack me up into little pieces, and every person on this boat would help him feed the fish.

Even knowing this, my mouth opened as his hand shot out. But my scream was cut off when he cupped my cheek, his hand gentle, as he tilted my face up to his. I realized suddenly that he was trembling. "Luca?"

"You're mine," he whispered as his head lowered and his lips brushed over mine, the tip of his tongue wetting my bottom lip. "Mine," he whispered again, so quietly I was unsure if he was talking to me or himself.

My lips parted on a moan, and his tongue swept into my mouth. I clutched his arms, feeling unsteady on my feet with the movement of the boat and the way he was kissing me like I was all he needed to survive and he was on death's door. His large hands came up to cup my face, holding me in place while he ravaged my mouth.

Breaking off the kiss with a groan, he pulled back just enough to focus on me, his eyes hungry as they traveled over my face. The cool air inside the cabin caressed my skin, and I shivered. "Don't fight me," he said, but it wasn't an order. More like a plea.

Slowly, he untied the top of my suit, unwrapping me like a precious gift. "What if someone comes in?" I asked.

"They wouldn't fucking dare."

I shivered again as he slid the straps over my shoulders and down my arms, leaving me naked from the waist up.

His hands slid up my ribcage and his thumbs brushed my hard nipples.

"So pretty," he murmured.

I didn't know how to handle this Luca. This man who was so gentle and reverent as he stripped me of my bottoms. I didn't know what to do. How to act. So I just stood there, my body trembling with an awakening desire until all of the anger and all of the mortification faded away as he kissed the scarred skin on my chest, working his way down to my breasts, where he ran his tongue around my sensitive nipples. His mouth covered every inch of my stomach, then he dropped to his knees as he went lower, kissing and licking the skin above my pubic hair, his hands on my hips to hold me still as he pressed his face into the curls and breathed deep.

My knees gave out, and I sat on the bed, my breaths coming hard and fast and my blood rushing to the surface, sensitizing my skin. Luca kissed my leg above the knee, then the other, spreading them wide as he worked his way higher up my thighs. He pulled me to the edge of the bed.

"Lie back, *amore.*"

I did as he asked, my hips lifting, searching for his mouth before he'd even touched me. And when the tip of his tongue licked through my folds and found my clit, I jerked, a cry wrung out of me, needing more.

With a deep groan, he gave me what I was asking for, sealing his mouth over my pussy as his tongue licked and tasted. He pulled me closer, looping my legs over his strong shoulders and lacing his fingers over my lower belly. I was trapped, unable to get away even if I wanted to.

My fingers gripped his hair, holding him to me as my orgasm crashed over me fast and hard, my body no longer in my control as it convulsed beneath him. His tongue moved down, entering me so he could lick up every last drop.

"Again," he growled against my sensitive skin. His mouth returned to me, not as hurried this time.

"Luca." His name left me on a needy breath.

"Mmm." His moan rumbled through me, igniting my nerve endings as I felt the first stirrings of desire move through me. He took his time, pulling away and blowing on my swollen clit, kissing my inner thighs, then returning to the place I wanted him most. And when I was writhing on the bed, the ache in my lower belly tightening and releasing with increasing speed, he unhooked his hands and slid one beneath my ass. Slowly, he slid his thumb inside of me, moaning as my body tightened around his finger.

"Luca, please," I begged.

I moaned in frustration when his thumb left me, only to catch my breath in surprise when he slid it into my ass just as his mouth covered me again, his tongue finding the perfect spot. I cried out as another orgasm took me by surprise, this one even harder than the last. His name was a prayer on my lips as his thumb pumped in and out of my ass and his tongue did wicked, delicious things to my cunt.

When I could breathe again, I opened my eyes to find him crawling over me, his cock hanging thick and heavy from the juncture of his hips. I thought he was bringing it to my mouth, but instead, he grabbed me under the arms, muscles flexing as he lifted me higher on the bed.

"You're mine," he said again as he pushed inside of me, his head falling to my shoulder. My body tightened around him, and he moaned. "Say it, Veda."

"I'm yours," I whispered.

He stilled inside of me and lifted his head to look me in the eye. "Say it again," he ordered.

The vulnerability I saw there made me want to weep. "I'm yours," I told him. And it was true. I couldn't fight it anymore.

Triumph lit his blue eyes and he started to move inside of me, each thrust more possessive than the last. He whispered in my ear as he claimed me. Scandalous things that made me arch into him and beg for more.

And when he came, I came with him, our cries mingling in the cool air of the cabin.

.   .   .

LUCA HELD my hand all the way back to the house, and more times than not, I'd glance over to find him looking at me with a bemused expression on his handsome face.

I knew exactly how he felt.

"I'm sorry I had to do that," he suddenly said. "I'm sorry I embarrassed you that way. It was the only way to get Gino off your scent."

"I'm not a dog," I told him.

"No, but he is. Once he sets his sights on something he wants, there's no deterring him until he has it. And he wanted you."

"Why?"

He let out a little laugh. "Why? What kind of question is that?" His eyes roamed over me, once again concealed beneath my coverup. "You're stunning, Veda. A woman through and through, but one who still has the slightest essence of innocence about her."

"Well, I won't have that for long hanging around with you."

Luca smiled and Enzo barked out a laugh from the front seat. "Sorry," he said. "Sorry," he repeated, focusing on the road.

"Anyway," Luca continued after he'd waved away his apology. "I apologize that I had to put you through that. Truly."

He was watching me, waiting for my reaction, and I saw a glimmer of uncertainty in his blue eyes that made my breath catch and my heart skip a beat. That I was the one who caused this powerful man to feel that gave me a heady sense of power, even as I immediately tried to console him. I squeezed his hand. "It's okay. I mean, it's not okay, but I understand."

The relief he felt was palpable. "When we get home, I need to speak to my men for just a few minutes and then the rest of the night I'm free. Will you wait for me?"

"Sure," I told him. "I'll see what Lisa packed us for dinner."

He brought my hand to his mouth and kissed the back of my knuckles as we pulled up to the house. I got out and walked around to the back to get the cooler. Enzo joined me, pulling it out and setting it on the ground while he closed the hatch. The others were already there, standing around the other SUVs while they waited for us.

"Enzo, I need you here," Luca told Enzo as he was about to lift the cooler and help me take it inside. Turning around, he waved one of the other guys over.

I started to protest as the one who'd cornered me in my old apartment came forward. "It's okay. I can carry it in myself."

"I know you can, but you won't," Luca told me. "Not while there're all of these strong, able-bodied males just standing around doing nothing."

Not knowing what else I could say to convince him without making myself look suspicious, I gave him a small smile and backed out of the way as his man came over to pick up the cooler. "I'll just be in the kitchen."

"I'll be there as soon as I can."

Still, I hesitated until Luca cocked his head in question. With no other way to avoid making a scene, I turned on my heel and marched into the house, Luca's man right behind me.

I nearly cried in relief when I saw Lisa was still there, drinking a cup of tea at the table, a notepad in front of her and a pen in her hand. She jumped up when we walked in. "How was the lake?" she asked with a smile.

"It was hot," I told her. "But nice." I lowered my eyes before she could see the lie in them. "We never even made it to our dinner," I explained as Luca's man set down the cooler.

"Oh! Well, here." Lisa jumped out of her chair and went right over to it. "Let me just get that going for you. Y'all must be starving."

Any other time I would have shoo'd her away, but there was no way in hell I was about to put myself into that position again. So I just smiled and thanked her as I stood awkwardly just inside the room, shifting my weight back and forth.

Luca's man gave Lisa a wave as she bent over the cooler, then headed my way, his eyes hard on my face. As he passed me, he smiled. "You have three days," he told me, too quiet for Lisa to hear. "You'd better have something for me." The "or else" didn't even need to be said. It was in his tone. "Enjoy your dinner," he said, louder this time. And then he was gone.

Three days. What the hell was I supposed to find out in three days? I stayed where I was until I heard the front door slam. Somewhere through the pounding of my pulse in my ears, I realized Lisa was talking to me. "I'm sorry, what?"

She gave me a look, but repeated what she'd said. "I said you look good. You got some sun."

"Oh, yeah." I tried to smile, but it didn't reach my eyes. "Kind of hard to avoid on the lake. But it felt good," I added. "Sorry, I didn't mean for that to come out sounding so snappy."

Lisa set foil packs on the island and turned on the oven behind her. "Are you alright?" she asked when she turned around. "You seem off. Did something happen with Luca?"

I felt my cheeks get hot. "I'm fine," I lied. "Just tired from being in the sun all afternoon."

"Well, why don't you sit down, and I'll get this dinner made so you can have something in your stomach."

I did as she suggested, taking a seat at the counter after she turned away my offer to help her. She always turned me down, and I still kept offering. It was strange to me to always have someone waiting on me. But tonight, I didn't argue with her as much as I normally would have. And as much as I would love to run upstairs and wash the lake water and sex off of me, I was afraid to venture off by myself, even though I'd heard the front door close behind him and knew he wasn't normally in the house.

Three days.

I had three days to dig up some dirt on Luca to give to Mario.

CHAPTER 23

VEDA

The days came and went, and I spent them in equal parts bliss and terror.

Ever since our excursion on the boat, Luca was different. And so was I, if I was going to be honest. It was like the rubber band of events that kept pulling me back to him had snapped, and this time—this time—I was with him because I wanted to be with him.

Because I was beginning to care way too much.

It wasn't because he was suddenly a sweet talker or anything like that. No, Luca was still the same fucked up, possessive asshole he'd always been. But something had changed. He never went more than a couple of hours before he'd find me in the house. And he always looked slightly panicked until he could touch me again.

And he was always touching me. If we were in the same room, he wanted me beside him, his hand wrapped around my hip, resting on my thigh, or tangled in my hair.

At night, in bed, after he'd tasted every inch of my body in the most delicious ways, he would pull me close and wrap his arms and legs around me, unable to sleep until I was cocooned against him, oftentimes with one hand cupped between my legs or gripping one of my breasts. I had the feeling he would soak me into his skin if he could.

It made me feel needed. Wanted. Safe. The game we'd been playing over. I was no longer a piece on the board he moved around according to his will, because he knew the stakes were too high. If he lost this time, he would lose me again. And this time, I wouldn't come back. He could force me to live here. He could take my body. But he would never have my heart again. Not like he did now.

Every look, every touch, every word was precious to me because with every second that ticked by, I knew our time was coming to an end. And I didn't want to waste it.

On the third day, I still hadn't been able to get any information for Mario. Of course, I hadn't really been trying either. I'd just been going through the moments, hoping some miracle would come along and save me from having to do it.

But nothing ever did.

With time running out, I became desperate. I had to get something, anything, to get Mario off my back and Luca off his radar.

Luca was in his gym working out, and I knew he'd be there for at least an hour, if not longer. Enzo was with him, and I hadn't seen Tristan all morning, so he must be off on some errand or maybe getting some down time. I normally joined Luca for at least some of that time to go over my self-defense lessons, but I'd bowed out today claiming I hadn't slept well last night.

This was my only chance.

My bare feet were silent on the hard floors as I hurried past the kitchen and down the hall toward Luca's office. Slipping inside, I quietly shut the door behind me, my heart pounding in my throat. Turning around, my eyes landed on his desk.

Taking a deep breath for courage, I hurried across the room and sat down in his chair. Ignoring the voice in my head that told me this was wrong, that I was betraying the man I cared about, I jiggled the mouse until the monitor came on. It was password locked, of course. "Shit."

I didn't even know where to start guessing what his password was. And it made me realize, I didn't even know when his birthday was. Or where he was born. Or anything about his life growing up. Did he have a pet? Did he like school? What kind of a boy was he? And would I be alive long enough to discover these things about him? Because I really, really wanted to.

Setting aside those kinds of thoughts, I started picking up papers on his desk, hoping I'd find something that would give any kind of a clue of the supposed deal Mario was wanting info on.

As I searched, I thought again about just telling Luca everything. But still, I hesitated. Luca didn't trust easily, and if I told him I'd been sent back to him as a rat to get information for his brother, he'll wonder why I'm just telling him now. Maybe he won't believe me when I tell him I was angry, and scared, and that up until a few days ago, a tiny part of me wanted to do it, to get back at him for everything he'd done to me. Maybe he'll think I've been reporting back to Mario all along.

And I knew what happened to people who crossed a man like Luca. It didn't matter how much he liked to fuck me. I'd end up just like my sister.

My adrenaline ran so high my hands were shaking and tears filled my eyes, blurring my vision. I found nothing on the desk that had any importance. Not even a random address or phone number, so I moved on to the drawers.

The center one had the usual pens, whiteout, paperclips and an assortment of sticky notes. I moved to the three larger drawers on the right. The top one held notepads and more odds and ends. The middle one was full of paper for the printer.

When I pulled on the third drawer, I found it was locked. I froze, trying to remember if I'd ever seen a key that might fit.

"If I were a mob boss, or whatever he is, where would I keep something like that?" The desk didn't give me any hints, but I wasn't expecting any. And besides, I think I knew. If I was a big, bad mafia guy, and I had secret files or whatever, I'd keep the key on me at all times.

Checking that everything was as I'd found it, I tiptoed across the office and put my ear to the door, listening for anyone who might be coming. When all was quiet, I cracked it open and peeked out. I heard Lisa rattling around in the kitchen, but otherwise no one was around. Hurrying now, I made it to the stairs without her seeing me and rushed up to Luca's room.

The slacks he'd worn today were folded neatly on a shelf in the closet with his gray button-down laid carefully over them, waiting for him to get finished with his workout. Disturbing them as little as possible, I started checking the pockets of his pants. They were all empty.

"Dammit!" I whispered.

Smoothing my hands over the material to make sure I didn't leave any wrinkles, I was torn between breathing a sigh of relief or sitting on the floor and freaking out when I felt something hard in the pocket of Luca's shirt. Reaching my hand inside, I felt cool metal and pulled it out.

A key.

I stood there staring at it, wondering if I was courageous enough or stupid enough to go back into Luca's office. I glanced over at the clock on the nightstand. I still had a good thirty minutes, at least, until Luca was done with his workout. Shoving the key into the pocket of my loose cotton shorts, I went back downstairs.

I made it back to the office with no one seeing me, and once again, I closed the door behind me. Hustling over to the desk, I sat down and inserted the key into the locked drawer. It fit perfectly. Turning it to the right until I heard a click, I left the key in the lock and pulled the drawer open.

It was full of hanging files. Pushing them back on the rails to give me some room, I pulled the first one forward and opened it up. Inside were a bunch of receipts. I pulled out the first one but couldn't tell what it was for. The total spent, however, was just over a thousand dollars. I put it back where I'd found it and went to the next folder.

"What are you doing in here, Veda?"

I jumped so violently, the top of my hand hit the underside of the second drawer and I cried out in pain. My eyes flew to the person who'd spoken as I held my injured hand protectively to my chest.

Tristan stood just inside the door, looking like he'd just came in from outside. He wore no jacket, just slacks and a dress shirt with the top buttons undone. A black shoulder holster stood out starkly against his white shirt, his gun within easy reach. I hadn't even heard him come in.

"Uh...I was just looking for something."

He planted his feet and waited.

Fuck. Fuck. Fuck! Desperately, I tried to think of something to tell him. Something that would make sense, but my mind was blank. I looked around him to the open doorway, but there was no way I'd get past him. Panic set in hard, and I swung around, looking for a way to open the window behind me. The fact that if I jumped, the chances were very likely I wouldn't survive didn't escape me. It was the coward's way out, but a much better alternative to my mind right at that moment.

"Luca, I need you to come to your office immediately."

I swung around just as Tristan slid his phone back into his pocket. "No! Tristan, please! I can explain!"

He crossed his arms over his chest and cocked his head, his expression completely neutral. There was no outrage. Not even a lot of curiosity. He was just doing his job, and I had the distinct feeling that if I was anyone else, he wouldn't just be standing there keeping me caged in the office until Luca got there. I had no doubt I would've felt a bullet by now. A wall of muscle and loyalty keeping me in here until his boss joined us.

Somewhere in the back of my mind, I realized my cheeks were wet, and I swiped at my eyes with the back of my hands. "I can explain," I told him again. "This isn't what it looks like."

"No? Because what it looks like is you snooping around Luca's office. It *looks like* you stole the key to the locked drawer and you're digging around in there trying to get information. Which can only mean you're working for somebody else. So, tell me, Veda? Am I wrong?"

Even though his voice was almost bored, his dark eyes were cold and hard, and I knew there was no way in hell I was going to get anywhere with him. I didn't know

Tristan as well as I knew Enzo, and honestly, they both scared the fucking hell out of me. But whereas Enzo was quite obvious about who and what he was, Tristan was something of an enigma.

We stood like that, staring at each other across the space of Luca's large office, when he walked in wearing nothing but a pair of loose, gray shorts almost identical to mine. There was sweat dripping down his temples, dampening his hair, and tape wrapped around his knuckles. Tristan stepped aside when he appeared, with Enzo right behind him in black running pants and a white tank top, missing his sunglasses, the black tattoos on his left shoulder on full display.

Luca visibly calmed when he saw me standing there with Tristan. "What's going on?" he asked as his eyes went back and forth between us.

"Do you want to tell him?" Tristan asked me. "Or shall I?"

"Please don't do this," I whispered to him. "Please, Tristan." I don't know why I bothered. It's not like the evidence wasn't right there for all to see. There was no way in hell I could talk my way out of this. All Luca had to do was walk around his desk and he would see me standing in front of his chair, the locked drawer still wide open beside me. But some mad, nonsensical part of me kept thinking that if I just kept denying it that somehow, I would live to see tomorrow.

Tristan stared back at me, not a speck of emotion on his handsome face, and waited.

My knees began to shake, and I reached behind me, blindly reaching for the arms of the chair. I found it just as my legs gave out and I sank into the plush leather. I couldn't take my eyes off of Tristan, mostly because I didn't want to look at Luca. I didn't want to see his face when Tristan told him what he'd caught me doing.

"Tristan, what's going on?" Luca repeated.

He nodded toward the desk.

I couldn't move, couldn't breathe, as Luca hesitated for a moment, his eyes going back and forth between me and Tristan. In my peripheral vision, I saw him walk toward me, around the desk, to stand on my left side as I sat frozen, my eyes straight ahead.

Luca was quiet for a long time. So very, very quiet. "Leave us," he finally said. "Go about your duties. I'll handle this."

Without hesitation, Tristan and Enzo left the office, closing the door firmly behind them. I cried out softly when I heard the latch click. Tears running down my face to drip into my lap, I waited for Luca to rage at me. To strike me. To do *something*. He stood so close I could smell his warm, masculine scent. Clean soap and dark spice and just the slightest hint of sweat.

But when he spoke, his voice was calm. Carefully controlled. "Why are you sneaking around, looking through things that are in a locked drawer?"

I didn't reply. I couldn't. My throat felt like it was closing up as silent sobs welled up inside of my chest until I thought my ribcage would burst.

"Veda, look at me."

But I couldn't. I couldn't! I knew what I would see there. Betrayal. Anger. Maybe hurt. Disgust. And I couldn't bear to see him look at me like that. I just couldn't. So, instead, I covered my face as the pressure in my chest burst forth and sobbed into my hands like the fucking coward I was. I wasn't cut out for this life. I couldn't take it. And he would never, ever, forgive me. Even if he let me live. He would never trust me again.

He'd never look at me the same way.

I heard something hit the desk in front of me. "Clean up your face and get yourself together. You're not leaving this office until I have answers."

Oh god. He sounded so...cold.

Still crying and sniffling, I lowered my hands to see a box of tissues on the desk in front of me. I pulled out a few and wiped my face and blew my nose, a welcome sense of numbness coming over me now that my initial panic attack was passing. When I was finished, Luca dropped down to his haunches beside me, resting one arm on the desk and one on the chair seat next to my thigh. His fingers played with the hem of my shorts.

"Veda, I need you to be honest with me and tell me what's going on." A spark of hope burned in my chest when I thought I heard a slight tinge of warmth. Enough to make me think that maybe he'd listen and let me explain.

I glanced over at him, gauging his expression, but it was carefully neutral, his blue eyes giving nothing away. "I'm so sorry," I told him. "I didn't have a choice."

"Sorry for what, exactly?"

"I had no choice," I repeated, my eyes pleading for him to understand. "I did it to protect you." I still sounded like I was on the edge of panic. I couldn't help it.

He cocked his head, much like Tristan had done. "What exactly did you do?"

"I thought I was safe, once I was back here. I thought he couldn't get to me. But he did. He did." A note of hysteria had entered my voice. "He found me in my apartment that day. And the other day when we went to the lake."

His eyes narrowed and I could see his sharp mind going through everyone who was with me those days. "Who did?"

"I don't know his name," I whispered. Then louder, because I couldn't lie to him, "He came into my room while I was in the closet packing my clothes. Enzo can tell you who he was."

He was quiet a moment while he thought about that. "And he was on the boat the other day?"

I nodded.

"No one spoke to you on the boat other than me."

There was note of disbelief in his tone, and I felt my chest crack wide open as my throat constricted. I barely managed to get the words out. "It was after we got home. He brought the cooler in."

A knowing expression bloomed on his face. "Okay," he said. "And who is he working for?" He cocked his wrist and his fingers brushed over my nipple. It hardened instantly as my breath caught. "Or do I even have to ask?"

"He works for Mario," I told him.

I shivered as the temperature in the room seemed to suddenly drop, even though Luca made no indication he'd even heard me.

Oh god. I was going to die.

CHAPTER 24
LUCA

"He works for Mario."

Veda's softly spoken words swirled round and round in my head, fighting for adherence. I wasn't surprised that my brother had turned one of my men. That was the way of things sometimes in my world. What I couldn't believe was Veda—my *vita*—would do this to me. "Why didn't you tell me all of this immediately?"

"He said he would kill my parents. He said he would kill *you*." She pressed the back of her hand to her mouth in an attempt to halt the sob that tore from her chest as new tears ran down her face.

"So you thought it was better to do as he asked? To sneak around and...what?" My upper lip twitched in a semblance of a snarl. "Get information for him?"

She stared at me with wide gray eyes, the color leached from her face, and didn't answer me.

My hands shook, and I clenched them into fists. Afraid I would strike her if I didn't put some distance between us, I rose to my feet and paced away. The air conditioner kicked on, the only sound in the sudden silence, but I barely felt the drop in temperature across my heated skin. I wanted to hit something. To scream and rage and break every goddamned piece of furniture in the room.

She'd betrayed me. My *vita*, my life, had betrayed me. To my fucking *brother*. Had it all been a ruse? Was she with him this entire time? Did she really have a twin sister? Or were they one in the same? Had it all been a lie? Just another way for Mario to fuck with my head? Birth records could be forged. People created out of this air. The government did it all the time.

It took every ounce of my self-control to keep my movements casual and my voice calm. I was afraid if I let myself explode, one of us wouldn't make it out of this room alive. And despite everything she was telling me, despite the words coming out of her dirty, lying, whoring mouth, I couldn't bring myself to willingly hurt her.

Because whoever this woman was, whoever she worked for, she was mine.

I made my way over to the liquor and poured myself a generous glass of the hardest stuff I had. I drank that one down and half of another, the weight of Veda's stare heavy on my back. Waiting to see what I would do. "What did he want you to find?" I asked, my back still to her.

Her voice, when it came to me, was husky with her tears. Or maybe it was just fear. "He wanted me to find out what I could about a deal you made that's supposed to happen in a few days."

"And what did you tell him?"

"Nothing," she said adamantly. "Because I haven't even tried to find anything. Not until today. And that's only because the clock is running out and I couldn't think of any other way to get out of doing it."

I finished my drink and poured another. Getting drunk wasn't going to do me any good right now, but maybe it would get me through this moment in time without shattering into a million pieces.

Glass in hand, I turned to face her. She looked so small sitting there in my oversized chair, the black leather a stark backdrop to her blonde hair and bright pink top. "You never thought to just tell me? To trust *me*?"

She was silent as she stared at me, then, in a strangled voice, "He swore he would kill you." She stood and started walking toward me with slow, jilted steps. At my look, she stopped after just a few feet. Her hands waved around in front of her as she tried to make me understand. "Luca, please listen to me. He told me if I didn't do it, he'd kill you. But at first, I thought I was safe. I thought we were safe, as long as we were here, where no one could get to you. But then...then I realized he was here. Right here. Not Mario, but the other guy. He doesn't work for you. He works for Mario. And I was so fucking scared." The tears that had never completely stopped filled her eyes again and ran down her blotchy cheeks as a sob tore through her.

I watched her fall apart in front of me, and took a sip of my drink as I fought the urge to go to her. To hold her. To tell her everything was going to be okay.

Because that was a lie. A big fucking lie. Nothing was ever going to be okay with us again.

"I was terrified he would get to you," she continued when she could speak again. "I was so fucking scared that I would walk in here one day and find you with a bullet in your..." She couldn't finish, great heaving sobs wracking her body as I watched from across the room.

I tried to understand her thinking, but right now, right here, I couldn't wrap my head around it. My thoughts were too fractured, wrapped in the pain of her betrayal.

"I just wanted to save you," she whispered.

The glass I was holding smashed against the wall beside her head and she ducked down to the floor with a cry and threw her arms over her head. Stalking over to her, I grabbed her by the hair with one hand and brought her to her feet, my vision gone red. She cried out in pain, her hands wrapping around my wrist to try to ease the pressure.

"Save me?" I laughed in her face. "You've done nothing but take from me from the moment I fucking met you."

My eyes wandered over her face, still stunning, even red with tears and wracked with pain. "You took everything," I repeated. "EVERYTHING! You stole my revenge from me. Stole any chance of me having a relationship with my father. You even wrapped my fucked up brother around your finger to the point he had to brand you to show everyone you were his!"

"Luca, please. You're hurting me!"

My mouth snapped shut, and I suddenly released her, feeling nothing as she fell to the floor at my feet. Pain flared within me, pain like I'd never felt before, wrapping its fingers around my throat until I had to strain to get the words out. "You act the victim so well, *amore*. All of that shit you told me about your time with Mario...they were lies, weren't they?"

She stared up at me in shock. "No," she told me. "I didn't lie, Luca."

"And why would I believe anything you say to me now? Why, Veda? When your bear the mark of my brother and I catch you spying in my office?"

Her jaw clenched, and her shoulders went back. "After everything we've been through, everything *you've* done to *me*, this is what you believe? Really?"

Cold, hard truth slapped me in the face, and for a moment I couldn't breathe. She was right. I'd been a fucking fool. "That's exactly why I believe it," I said out loud.

She blinked, and some of the steel slipped out of her spine.

I took a step toward her. Stopped. "I'm not a good man, Veda. I know this. Yet you took this cold, dead heart of mine and made it beat again. For you, Veda. All for you. I let you in. Let you know me. And you *betrayed* me."

She reached for me across the space between us, her face crumbling as fresh tears streamed down her cheeks. "Luca." Her voice cracked. "I love you."

Her words stabbed through me, opening fresh wounds that I feared would never heal. Because they were too late. I closed the distance between us and took her face in my hands as I searched for the storms in her eyes. But they weren't there. There was only fog and shadows. With a growl, I took her mouth hard, bruising her lips as I poured every fucked up thing I was feeling into the kiss. And when I broke it off, she knew.

"You love me?" I asked her.

She tried to nod her head, but I still held it between my palms. I could crush it so easily. So fucking easily. "Yes," she whispered.

Leaning down, I licked the seam of her mouth, then kissed my way up to her ear. "Then RUN," I told her. "You have thirty minutes."

I dropped my hands and backed away as the walls crashed down around my heart and ice filled my veins. It was comforting, in a way, to go back to being the man I was before I knew her. I knew this man well, and he did what he had to do to survive.

Veda's eyes searched my face. Searching. Searching. Always searching. But whatever she found made her suck in her breath in terror. Without a word, she spun around and ran for the door. Flinging it open, she ran past Enzo and Tristan, and I heard her bare feet on the hard tiles of the great room.

"Let her go," I told them when they looked at me in question. Turning away, I walked across the broken glass to pour myself another drink, leaving bloody footprints on the way. I didn't feel the shards slicing the bottoms of my feet. I didn't feel anything. "Enzo."

I heard him come into the office. "Yeah."

"Take her out of this house. Give her enough money to go wherever she wants to go. Bus. Plane. I don't give a shit. Make sure I can't track her."

"I'm on it."

He left, closing the door behind him.

I walked back across the glass to my chair and sat down in the silence, my hands gripping the arms tight enough to hold me there. A few minutes later, I heard the front door close.

And the last remnants of my heart shattered.

~

Read the conclusion of Luca and Veda's story in
His Win.

ACKNOWLEDGMENTS

As always, I need to thank my wonderful husband, Joe, for always being my biggest supporter as I venture into this new to me genre. I love you, Joe Joe. <3

My bestest author friend, Isabel Jordan, for being my alpha beta reader, talking me off the ledge, always being available to commiserate with me with all of this hard authoring stuff, and holding my hand through blurb hell.

Angel's Army, my ARC team, you all are awesome! Thank you for all of your patience and hanging with me. Your support means the world to me!

And to all of you readers who took a chance on His Game, a brand new dark romance by a new to you author! I can never express how grateful I truly am.

ABOUT THE AUTHOR

Hi! My name is Angel Rayne and I write dark, delicious romance with antiheroes who would burn down the world to save the woman they love. I never understood why the villains never win the girl, and so I decided to write them their own love stories where they do.

Here are a few other odds and ends about me...

-Music inspires my stories and I make playlists for every book.

-I am not a fast writer. My stories take time to write. They need to brew in my head. To have book releases close together I have to write ahead. But I would much rather take the time the stories need to be the best they can be than try to rush them out. Trust me on this one.

-I love the rain, and I'm happiest when I'm sitting in a coffee shop with my laptop as it storms outside.

-I prefer to go watch movies alone, with one of those fancy coffees hidden in my purse. (Yes, I really do this.)

-My husband calls me his "little bird" because anything that sparkles catches my eye.

-I will never have enough soft blankets. Ever.

-I love ALL THE DRAMA...but only in books.

-I will forever re-watch The Phantom of the Opera with the hope that by some miracle, this time Christine will choose the right guy.

Thank you for reading my stories, and I always love to hear from you! You can reach me at: angel@angelrayne.com